THE LEGEND OF TARIK

Also by Walter Dean Myers

THE BLACK PEARL & THE GHOST
FAST SAM, COOL CLYDE, AND STUFF
THE GOLDEN SERPENT
IT AIN'T ALL FOR NOTHIN'
MOJO AND THE RUSSIANS
THE YOUNG LANDLORDS

The
LEGEND
of TARIK

Walter Dean Myers

The Viking Press
New York

815916

First Edition
Copyright © by Walter Dean Myers, 1981
All rights reserved
First published in 1981 by The Viking Press
625 Madison Avenue, New York, New York 10022
Published simultaneously in Canada by Penguin Books Canada Limited
Printed in U.S.A.
1 2 3 4 5 85 84 83 82 81

Library of Congress Cataloging in Publication Data
Myers, Walter Dean,   The legend of Tarik.
Summary: After witnessing the annihilation of his
people by El Muerte's legions, young Tarik undergoes the
training which will enable him to destroy this fierce leader.
I. Title.
PZ7.M992Le   [Fic]   80-27655   ISBN 0-670-42312-2

TO DR. EDWARD W. ROBINSON, JR.,
A FRIEND AND A TEACHER

THE LEGEND OF TARIK

PART ONE

ONE

IT CAME TO PASS, FOUR GENERATIONS AFTER THE MESsage of the prophet had reached the ears of men, that the family of Kwesi Ntah found itself on hard times. They were merchants, trading in dyes near the highlands west of the River Niger. But when the wars between the followers of Bilal and the followers of the Christians closed the caravan routes to the east, all trade became impossible. Ntah watched as things went from bad to worse until finally he knew that he would have to move his family. It was either this or watch them starve. And so, on the first new moon after the feast of the Two Moons, Ntah moved his family, which included his wives, Ime and Opari, and their three sons, Mato, Tarik, and Umeme.

They traveled northward until they reached the place called Oulata. There was good trading at Oulata, and Ntah felt that there would be a place there for his family. He built a home in the middle of a stand of wild olive trees and was greatly pleased by what he had done. But still, in the evenings, he would gaze off into the distance whence he came and the lands familiar to him and to his fathers before him.

There was much trade in gold at Oulata. As was the custom, those who would trade their wares brought them to the place of silent barter and left them there for weights of gold. Here Ntah brought his dyes, leaving them for the silent traders of Oulata, who would take them and leave gold where the dyes had been. So it was for nearly two years that Kwesi Ntah lived and kept his family in peace and tranquillity.

Then one day, like the brooding of an ugly storm that sweeps from the mountains, talk of war darkened the sun of Oulata. Many fled, as they had earlier from the highlands and from the other places in Alkebu-lan that the war had touched. But the silent traders of Oulata did not flee, nor did Kwesi Ntah.

The noises of war, echoed at first only on the lips of those who had not seen its consequence, now came close to Oulata. Ntah, a man of stubborn pride, tried to lift himself above the war, even as an eagle lifts itself above the tops of mountains to catch the stirring wind. But the warriors from the north who came upon Oulata cared for neither man nor eagle. It was said that the fierce leader who swept through the cities and the villages, killing all who dared oppose him, was the son of the son of the son of Genseric. When this was said, it was done with trembling lips; such was the history of that noted family. The invading army reached Oulata, and there was none who opposed it. The people did not dare show their naked faces to the conquerors, but bowed their heads as they passed by. The leader of the warriors who fell upon Oulata was Artia Akwara. But he was not called by this name. Rather, he was called El Muerte, first by his warriors and then by all men.

It was said that El Muerte slept always alone, for any living thing that spent the night with him would be dead in the morning, such was his evil. Nor was there a living thing that he loved, or beauty that he would not destroy. This was what came to Oulata, calling itself a man.

At first the people of Oulata resisted, but they were no match for the ferocity of El Muerte's warriors. Finally the chiefs called upon the people to cease their resistance before they were all killed.

On the day that the people of Oulata laid down their weapons and brought forth their goods to pay homage to their conquerors, the sun did not shine. The sky was the color of old silver, and ravens circled high above the city. The circling ravens were a bad omen, Ntah thought. That morning, before the night had given up its darkness, a stork had been found dead in front of a holy place. That, too, was a bad omen.

When the people of Oulata had spread their homage upon the ground in front of El Muerte, he was not satisfied.

"Slaves!" he shouted. "Slaves and more gold!"

The people of Oulata shrank back in terror. The chiefs spoke among themselves. Was not death better than slavery? To go off with El Muerte was beyond the reaches of the heart. And so again they lifted their arms to defend themselves. But it was of no use. The warriors of El Muerte, many times those of Oulata in number, and without mercy, cut them down like so many stalks of grain. Those who were not killed were taken captive. And so it was that Ntah was taken captive, along with his son Umeme and his son Tarik. The other son, Mato, along with his wives, was killed in the battle of Oulata.

The journey to the land of El Muerte was the most difficult that Ntah had ever taken, for every step was made heavy with grief, every breath laden with despair. He and his sons made the long trek from Oulata, their hands tied behind their backs, the whips of their captors cracking across their black shoulders. When they had traveled the better part of three full moons, they reached the Strait of Hercules and crossed it on small boats, bound hand and foot. On land again, they traveled farther until Ntah thought that he could walk no longer. His strength gone, his legs moved from memory.

When they reached a place called Encina, they stopped and were put into a large compound. It was the first time in all the time of their captivity that Ntah had had a chance to speak to his sons. He sought to bring them comfort but could bring them only his sorrow. He did not speak at length to them, nor was the timbre of his voice like the drum. He spoke to them only in quick whispers, offering but a few words of comfort, for his heart was breaking at the sadness and despair in their eyes.

On the fourth day of their stay in the compound they were made to lay off a great ring of cedar branches. When they had done this, under the blows and whips of their captors, they were again put into the compound. From where they stood behind the walls of the compound they could see many people gather around the ring. Some of them were dressed finely, while others were obviously warriors. It did not take long before they saw where the wind would carry their fate.

Three of El Muerte's men came among them and took the young maidens and the young men. These they brought before one of the finely dressed men, who sat in a high chair outside the ring they had constructed. He nodded his approval, and the young captives were bound and taken away. Then another man was taken into the center of the ring. He was given a long pole with which to defend himself. Presently a warrior on a horse entered the ring and charged the man, bearing down on him with a lance. The startled man had no chance, and soon lay dead in the center of the ring.

There was a great cry of approval from the people who watched, and they held up colored cloths. Then another man was led into the ring. He was an old man and was given a pole, as had the first. A horseman entered the ring and dispatched him with one blow of his sword.

And so it went, as the remaining captives from Ntah's tribe were taken to the arena and killed for sport. And then it became the turn of Ntah, and his sons called out to him and tried to break through the walls of the compound. But it was no use. Ntah was not given a pole to defend himself with, but a sword. All eyes watched as Ntah stood in the center of the ring.

A silence fell among them, stilling both lip and limb. Then there were the sounds of hoofbeats, and a giant of a man on a huge white horse came slowly toward Ntah.

"El Muerte!" The whispered name rustled through the crowd like wind through autumn leaves.

The man was dressed in silver armor, but wore nothing on his head. His hair was dark and fell about his face like seaweed about a huge white shell. The horse walked proudly, stopping now and again, seemingly without command from the rider. The slitted eyes of the rider never left the black figure that stood alone in the ring. When he had come within the length of four men to where Ntah stood, the horseman withdrew his own sword from its scabbard and held it high above his head. It caught the sun and glistened as if it were alive. Then, suddenly, the horse charged and the sword came crashing down. To ward off the blow, Ntah lifted the sword he had been given, but it was broken in two by the sword of the horseman.

The horse stopped a few feet past Ntah and wheeled sharply. The sword was lifted again. Another charge, and Ntah lifted the broken sword to ward off the blow. The horse, when it had passed Kwesi Ntah, did not wheel but stood with his back toward him.

"El Muerte!" The name came from the crowd again.

Ntah slowly turned toward the compound. Blood poured from the side of his head and neck as he tried to take a step toward the place that held his sons. He fell noiselessly to the ground.

"El Muerte!"

Finally all the boys were pushed into the ring. Some of them cowered in fright. Others wept and pleaded for their lives. One of Ntah's sons went to the place where his father had fallen, and knelt there, cradling the lifeless body, staining his dark fingers with the blood of his father.

"Tarik!"

Tarik looked up. It was his younger brother, Umeme. The boy trembled with fear. Tarik had hardly lifted a hand to his brother when the horses were upon them. There were screams and blood as the soldiers rushed their horses through the group of boys. Their swords made a rushing noise through the air. Tarik found himself nearly lifted from the ground by a blow from the back. There was no time to move or to know what had happened to him. Only a great pain, and a greater darkness.

TWO

TARIK HEARD THE VOICES LONG BEFORE HE RECOG-
nized them as such. The pain in his head pushed in-
ward until he thought he could stand it no longer, and
still it continued. For a long time he lay still, not knowing
if he was dead or alive, or even if it mattered. He tried to
move his arm, and he could feel the hard ground beneath
him. He was afraid to open his eyes, but as the voices
came nearer he was even more afraid not to open them.

It was dark, and he could see only a few feet in front of
him. He could not tell where the voices were coming
from. He tried to lift his head, and the pain became worse.
With all the strength he could muster, he lifted himself
to one elbow. There were small lights flashing in his eyes,
and he became dizzy.

"Here's one!" someone said.

He tried to turn, and the darkness once again enveloped
him.

When he awoke again, he was on a bed and in a warm
place, bathed with a soft glow of light from a lamp, and

smelling of the heady scent of the incense that had been mixed with the lamp's oil. It seemed at first to be a large cave, but as Tarik's eyes grew accustomed to the light he saw that it was a room in a building. The walls were made of yellow stone, except for the doorway, which was edged in red stone, its graceful curves mirroring those of the high vaulted ceiling.

The floor and the hearth were made of the same kind of dark rough stone, but whereas the hearth was roughhewn, the floor had been polished and worn with age.

On one wall there was a coarsely woven fabric whose colors had long since faded, and which was stained at the top from the smoke of many oil lamps.

"Life must be very dear to you." A voice came from across the room.

There was a dark patch against the far wall, and a hazy figure moved within it. It was one of the pale ones!

Tarik tried to swing his legs over the side of the bed on which he was lying, but they would not move. He looked down at them, his heart pounding. They were not tied, but still he could not move them.

"Do not be afraid," the man said, coming over to him. "If I had wished to do you harm, I could have done so easily during the days and nights you have been lying there. Now lie back and calm yourself."

It was an old man. His face was round and pink, and there were great sags under his chin. He had no hair on his head, and the hair of his brows was gray. His face was flat and somewhat bigger than one would have imagined from his body, which was slight and bent with age.

Tarik tried to move again, this time more slowly, and found that he could do so but only with great difficulty. Still, he managed to sit up.

The man offered him bread and a warm liquid in a bowl, and Tarik ate and drank. The food filled his body with warmth, and he again tried to move, this time to stand. He was halfway up when he fell back on the bed.

"You have suffered much, little brother," the man said. "And you will suffer even more, I fear. But for now rest. There will be time enough for all that is to come."

Tarik wanted to ask him questions, to speak to him and show him that he was not helpless. But he lay back on the small bed instead, and was soon asleep.

When he awoke again, there was no pain in his head. He managed to sit up but could feel the weakness in his limbs. He thought of the times that his father had given him heavy burdens to carry and his arms had grown weary—

"My father!" His voice was hoarse. He looked around for his garments and saw them on a stool. He was putting them on when the man he had seen two days before came in.

"Ah, I see that you are up and about," the man said.

"I will be about my business," Tarik said. "I must find my family."

"God has given you no reason for haste, I fear," the man said. "For if your family was among those brought from the land of the blacks, then they are dead. I am sorry. Are you from Melli?"

For a long time Tarik could not speak. Words would

14

come to his throat only to die there. There was a memory, the sight of a thin black hand lifted against the sky, a hand that could not stop the terrible blow that rushed against it. Tarik closed his eyes against the pain. When he could speak again, it was to call the name of his brother.

"I do not know the word," the man said.

"My brother!" Tarik said. "Umeme is my brother! He was with me."

"Then he, too, is slain," the man said.

Tarik took a deep breath and fought back the grief that flooded his chest and filled his eyes with the sting of tears. He clenched his fists and closed his eyes, but he could not overcome the weakness that made his legs shake, and so he sat down.

"Weep," the man said. "Do not hold your pain within you. I will leave you now. Know that I have spoken the truth. Those who were with you are dead. Only you remain. Only you have witnessed what has happened to your people."

The sun, which shone through the high window, fell beneath the ledge, and the darkness gathered about Tarik and chilled him to the very bone. All night he lay curled upon the small bed, torn first between tears and disbelief, and later between tears and sleep. And when the sun came through the window again the next morning, he had wrapped himself in a veil of silence. The pale man came again, bringing food, but Tarik did not touch it.

When the man returned, he looked at the food and at Tarik, and then he sat down.

"My name," he said, "is Ovolli Docao. I am an old

15

man, as you can see. When your people were brought here, I knew what would happen to them. I have seen it before. Some were taken to the arenas in the city, and some were taken to the ring. Those taken to the ring were killed that very day. It is the sport of the soldiers, something they learned from the East, I think. When the killing was over, I went among the bodies and buried those that were dead, and I found you. You were left for dead and were more so, perhaps, than alive.

"You have lost much, I know. I, too, have lost much. May I share my pain with you? Perhaps it is better to do so now, while your heart is too full of your own grief to be burdened with mine. For it is not to your heart that I address myself, but to the spirit within you.

"I have spent many years spreading the word of my God. I did not think of things that concerned most men, and one day I woke to find myself past the prime of my life. It was not a thing to worry about, for no man lives forever. But in this, the evening of my life, I took upon myself the joys and burden of a wife. And from this union I was granted, by the grace of God, a son. My joy lasted several months until the shadow of the man they call El Muerte fell across my path. I dared to stand in his way as he took without mercy from even the poorest of my people. I dared to speak against him as he did his unspeakable evils. It was he who, angered by my ill-considered moment of strength, dispatched my wife and child to the same darkness that he has now dispatched your father and loved ones.

"But where did this strength come from, this instant of

courage that led me to lose that which I held most dear beside the Lord? It was the memory of my own youth, perhaps rekindled by the birth of the child. For in my youth I was not a priest, but Docao the soldier and might have stood against him. Now I have only this to remind me of my folly."

The man held up his right arm to reveal a stump where his hand had been.

"It does not return my father to me," Tarik said.

"No, it does not," Docao continued. "Death calls every man, and at some time or another we must all listen.

"But let us dwell upon the living, shall we?" he continued. "There is another of your people who traveled this way years ago. He is a scholar. Once he looked upon the face of El Muerte at the same time that a cloud crossed the sun, and a shadow fell between them. El Muerte considered it a deliberate, malicious act. We see in the world around us that which we see in ourselves—is that not true?"

Tarik did not answer.

"Well, because of this provocation, El Muerte had the scholar seized and had his eyes put out. The man's name is Nongo, and it is he who has taught me the language of your people. We share the last days of our lives like two old snakes with only one hole.

"I thought that you would die, but Nongo thought you might live. I said to him that it was more hope than intellect that envisioned your survival. But look, you are alive, and even I have hope now." Docao stopped abruptly. "What are you called?"

"I am called Tarik."

"It will do," Docao answered. "Now you must get some rest."

The old man came again to Tarik in the morning. This time the man of whom he had spoken, Nongo, came also.

"It is good to know that you live," Nongo said.

Tarik looked at the man. His face was black, and although he seemed in most aspects old, his skin was smooth. There was a cloth around his head that covered his eyes.

"I am alive," Tarik said.

"And what is it that you wish from life, my brother?" Nongo said. He did not move as he spoke, but sat perfectly still. Nor did he raise his voice above that which could barely be heard.

"I wish to avenge the death of my family," said Tarik, "and the deaths of my people."

"Those are strong words," Nongo said, "and brave. But they are still words, with less weight upon the air than the smallest sparrow. Docao has used these words many times, and I have felt them reverberate within the chambers of my own heart. But I can see only visions of things past, and it is not enough. And Docao can lift no weapon against the man except knowledge."

"I have both eyes and hands," Tarik said firmly. "And the will to use them!"

"The hand can be easily trained," Docao said. "The young eye can be taught to see . . . but without the spirit only death awaits your efforts."

"I have the spirit!" Tarik said, standing.

"We will see," Docao said. "We will see."

Docao stood up and left the room. When he had gone, Tarik looked again at Nongo.

"Tell me of your home." Nongo spoke the words carefully, forming them in his mouth as if they were words spoken of a dear one. "Tell me what river ran by your village, and of the trees, and of the fruits."

"The river was the River Niger," Tarik said. "We lived a day and a half above Lake Debo. Sometimes I would go to see my mother's people, who were fishermen. They asked my father to let me stay and learn fishing, and my father said he would think about it, but I did not think he would do such a thing."

"Was your mother pleased that you might join her people?"

"No, she was not pleased. She wept and made me sit next to her," Tarik said. "My father said that if he let me go she would have no heart to beat and he would lose both wife and son."

"And what did your mother say?"

"She told him to eat his fou-fou before it grew cold." Tarik smiled. "It was the way she spoke when she was pleased. It did not matter if there was fou-fou to be eaten or not."

"Did you want to be a fisherman?" Nongo asked.

"I wanted to do the thing that was my father's trade," Tarik answered. "What is there to fishing but the same thing each day?"

"It is easier to watch than to do, my friend. Fish do not want you to catch them."

"I could do as well as the others my age," Tarik said. "They knew more than I, but I am as quick as anything that calls itself fisherman."

"And when you were not visiting your mother's people or helping your father in his trade, what did you do then?"

"The things that a man does," Tarik answered.

"The things that a man does?" repeated Nongo. "This thing pushes its way even through the pain?"

Tarik was puzzled. "What meaning do you put to my words?" he asked.

"Do not concern yourself with the meanings of old men," Nongo said. "We have seen truth from so many sides we often forget its face. Tell me, you know fishermen, have you known hunters as well?"

"Of course. People who would eat must have hunters about them."

"And did the fishermen fill their hearts with anger for the fish?" Nongo asked. "Did the hunters hate their prey?"

"No." Tarik looked into Nongo's face but could read nothing there as the old man nodded to himself. Then, thinking that perhaps Nongo had not heard him, he repeated his response. "No."

"Little brother, who comes from a land of sunshine and cool lakes and rivers that give him their fish, whose mother gave him nothing but warmth from her bosom, who saw in the footsteps of his father a noble path to follow, little brother." Nongo reached out until he had touched Tarik and then ran his rough fingers down the smooth line of Tarik's arm until he had found his hand. He took Tarik's hand in his own as he spoke.

"Little brother, what would you say if I told you that there should be no anger in your heart for the man who killed your father?"

Tarik tore his hand away.

"Then I would say that you are a fool!" Tarik spat the words through clenched teeth.

"Am I a fool?" Nongo asked. "There is a basin of water near the head of your bed. Do you see it?"

"I see it."

"Cup your hands like this and scoop up some of the water," Nongo said, holding his own hand in front of his blind face.

"I have done it," Tarik said.

"Then pour the water from one hand to the other as you speak the name of this man who has killed your father."

Tarik said in a low voice, "El Muerte. El Muerte. El Muerte." His hands trembled with rage as he spilled the water from his one hand to the other. Some of the water went into the newly cupped hand and the rest spilled on the floor.

"It is not easily done when the heart is angry, is it?" Nongo said.

"How did you know that I did not do it?" Tarik asked, his voice trembling. "You cannot see."

"No," Nongo said, "but I still hear the anger in your voice, and I know it is the anger that controls your hand. Before you face your enemy you must rid yourself of all hatred and anger. For hatred will make your eyes as blind as mine. It will make your limbs move when they should be still. It will make you cry out when you should be

21

silent. The man who has killed your father is no ordinary man," Nongo continued. "He is a man with much power and much skill. Some say that there is an evil within him that is larger than his body. To defeat such a man you must learn much, Tarik. Are you willing to learn?"

"I am willing," Tarik said.

Nongo told Tarik to take another handful of water and say what he had said before.

"I do not wish to say such a thing," Tarik said.

"Then go among the bulrushes and hide your tears," Nongo said, "for it is all that you will be capable of doing."

Tarik looked at the water in his cupped hand. "It was El Muerte who kill . . . who killed my father," he said. His hand shook as he said it, and much of the water spilled on the floor.

"Each morning," Nongo said, "you must reach into this basin and take a handful of water and say those hateful words, passing the water from hand to hand. When you can do this one hundred times and still have water to put back into the basin, you will then be ready for further training."

Each morning Tarik would rise and take a handful of water and speak the words as Nongo had instructed. Sometimes he would be able to do it the first time and not the second, and sometimes he would be successful ten times but not the next. Sometimes he would be almost up to a hundred before the anger would well up within him and the water would spill from his hands. Finally, after the moon had grown full again twice, he was able to complete the task, and went to Nongo.

"Nongo," he said, "look, I am master of my anger."

Slowly he took a handful of water, and, repeating each time that it was El Muerte who had killed his father, he passed the water from hand to hand one hundred times and then returned it to the basin without spilling a drop.

"It is done!" Tarik said boldly.

"No," Nongo answered, "it is not done, but it is well begun."

Tarik could see that Nongo was pleased with him and asked if there were other tasks for him to perform as well.

"It is good that you do not let your anger control the flow of your life," Nongo said. "But you must also come to understand the flow of life through all creatures and things. Come with me."

Nongo led Tarik out of the room in which he had been living and into a large garden. The garden had few flowers but many kinds of bushes and tall grasses that varied subtly in color from the pale green of clear shelf water to the deep blue of the morning sky before the sun has risen. The bushes were cut in the form of animals that seemed to lie casually about, and the grasses were in the shape of large flowers, with the dark grasses appearing to be the underside of the flowers, and the lighter being the uppermost petals, giving the illusion of great depth when they were indeed flat.

There was a thick entanglement of vines and trees at the edge of the garden. They served as a wall but allowed a mottled array of sunlight through the branches and leaves that fell alongside a small stream. Nongo knelt beside the stream and put his hand into the water. He bade Tarik to do likewise and to tell him what he felt.

"I feel the force of the water against my hand," Tarik said.

"It is the life in the water that you feel," Nongo said. "There is but one life, and it flows through all things. When it flows through the water, it is easy to feel. As it flows through the stone it is harder for us to feel. But even as a man can shape the stone to bring beauty to life, so he can shape anything he touches to control his own fate. You must learn to feel this flow of life, Tarik, that has flowed through all your ancestors and now flows through you. Go back to your room and feel the flow of life in the cup from which you drink. When you begin to understand that the cup was not born in your hands, then you will understand the cup. Feel the flow of life in the walls about you and of the one who put those walls in place. They say that objects are created, that people are born. That is not true, Tarik. Nothing is created or born, nothing falls away or dies. Nor is there a form or stick that has not lived before. When all this is known to you, no man can surprise you, for when you know the forces of his life, you will know all that is needed to stand against him."

Tarik went to his room, and each day he held in his hands the cup from which he drank. He touched the walls of his room, letting his fingers feel their roughness. And after a long while he began to feel that they were more than walls and that the cup was more than a cup. Even as his hands traced the roundness of the cup, he felt the hands that had made them round. Even as he felt the straightness of the walls, he felt the hands of the one who had made the walls straight. And when he had done these things, Tarik touched the chair with its carved lion shoulders, and he could feel the man who had carved them there, and with each thing in his room he did this. And when he had finished, he went back to Nongo and told Nongo what he had done.

Nongo nodded and said to him that it was good and said that now he was ready to be trained.

THREE

THE TRAINING OF TARIK BEGAN IN THE GARDENS OF Shange, which is where Nongo and Docao made their home. It was Docao who woke him the first morning of his training, but it was Nongo who waited for him in the gardens after he had washed himself.

"Good morning, little brother." Nongo sat cross-legged in the center of the gardens.

"Good morning, Nongo," Tarik answered. "I am ready to begin my training."

"That is good," Nongo said. "Come sit by my side."

This Tarik did, shivering slightly against the chill of the morning. For a long time Nongo did not speak, nor did Tarik. He knew that Nongo would speak when the time came to do so.

As Tarik sat, he thought that he saw something move against one of the walls that enclosed the gardens. He peered into the shadows but saw nothing. He dismissed the thought from his mind, but then again he thought he saw a movement. It looked as if there were someone standing in the shadows, a person smaller than Docao. Tarik wished to ask Nongo about this person, but waited patiently for the old man to speak. Eventually Nongo lifted his hand and began.

"Tarik." Nongo spoke slowly. "There are many things that a warrior must do if he is to be truly great. But there are three things that he must be able to do if he is to survive. I will tell you a story, and you will tell me the lesson it teaches.

"Once a blind man traveled down the road to a large city. He carried with him a small purse of silver with which to buy the goods he needed. As he traveled, he soon came upon three small boys, the sons of thieves and pirates. No sooner did they see him than they set upon him. They surrounded him and poked at him with sticks, looking for an opportunity to seize his purse. The blind man, who carried a great oaken staff, swung at the sound of their voices but could not hit them. Soon he was tired, and they were able to snatch his purse and flee.

"Now, Tarik, tell me what you have learned from this story."

"I have learned that one must see to defend one's self," Tarik said. "If the blind man could have seen, he could have beaten off the robbers."

"This," Nongo said, "is one of the things that can be learned. Can you see, Tarik?"

"Yes," Tarik answered. "I have my eyes."

"I hear the sound of a bird," Nongo said. "Tell me what it does."

Tarik looked at the orange tree in which sat a bird. As

he looked, the bird flew from the tree to the ground.

"There was a bird in the orange tree," Tarik answered. "Just now he flew from the tree to the ground."

"And tell me," Nongo said, "where does he put his feet when he flies?"

"His feet? I did not see his feet, Nongo."

"Ah, that is a pity," Nongo said. "You saw the bird for a moment on the tree, and then you saw the movement of a shape, and then you saw the bird on the ground. But you did not see the bird as he flew."

"What does it matter?" Tarik asked. "It could have been only the bird that moved. Nothing else sat on the tree."

"In battle," Nongo answered, "it is what a man does not see that kills him. It is the unwatched sword that starts high in the air and is suddenly upon him. It is the arrow that comes from nowhere and strikes him. It is the spear that finds the secrets of his life and spills them onto the ground.

"If you wished to capture the bird before it reached the ground, you would have been unable to. If the bird had been a sword aimed at your breast, you would have been slain. Tell me, Tarik, now what does the bird do?"

Tarik watched as the bird hopped from place to place, and then watched it as it suddenly lifted its wings and flew to the edge of a small fountain in the middle of the garden. This time he saw that it tucked its feet beneath it as it did so.

"It has flown to the fountain. As it flew, it tucked its

feet beneath it," Tarik said, feeling pleased with himself.

"And to which side did it turn its head as it landed?" Nongo asked quietly.

Tarik did not answer, for he had not seen this. Nor did he move when Nongo stood and put his hand upon his shoulder.

"Tomorrow," Nongo said, "perhaps we will be able to tell if your blindness is curable."

With these words Nongo left the gardens. Tarik's face burned with shame. Nongo, who was without eyes, had called him blind. For the rest of the day he sat in the gardens and watched the birds, seeing how they flew, how they turned their heads, how they moved the feathers in their tails, and how they turned to catch the sun.

He sat from morning until sunset, watching each movement in the gardens, watching each blade of grass move, watching field mice scurry along the edges of the walks.

Just as the sun set, he thought he saw a figure appear at the edge of the gardens and then quickly disappear. This time it looked like a young person, but it had appeared and disappeared so quickly that he could not be sure. He sat in the gardens until night fell, and then he went to bed.

"Let me tell you a story, Tarik," Nongo announced after Tarik had found him sitting in the gardens the next morning and sat next to him.

"One time a blind man traveled down the road to a large city. He carried with him a small purse with which to buy the goods he needed. As he traveled, he soon came upon three small boys, the sons of thieves and pirates. No sooner did they see him than they set upon him. They surrounded him and poked at him with sticks, looking for an opportunity to seize his purse. The blind man, who carried a great oaken staff, swung out but could not hit them. Soon he was tired, and they were able to snatch his purse and flee.

"Now, Tarik, tell me what you have learned from this story."

"I have learned that one must see to defend one's self," Tarik answered, as he had the day before.

"This is the lesson that any man could learn," Nongo said. "What else have you learned?"

Tarik thought for a long time. He tried to think what he would have done if he had been the blind man.

"The blind man should have swung at the sound of their voices," Tarik said.

"Yes," Nongo said. "That is another thing to be learned. Not only could he not use his eyes, he could not use his ears, either. Tell me, Tarik, can you use your ears?"

"Yes," Tarik replied. "I can use my ears, Nongo. I hear the birds singing, I hear you speak to me, I even hear the sounds of crickets in the tall grass."

"Do you hear the sound of your heart beating?"

Tarik listened. He heard the sounds that came from without his body, but nothing that came from within.

"No," he said to Nongo, "I do not."

"It is said"—Nongo spoke almost in a whisper—"that the footstep of death is exactly as loud as the sound of one heartbeat. When you can hear the sound of your beating heart, then you will be able to hear the approach of death as well."

Tarik, after Nongo had left, sat listening in the garden for the sound of his own heartbeat. It was not an easy task, for he had less occasion to use his ears than his eyes. At first he heard nothing, then he began to hear the sounds about him—the soft rustle of the wind through the trees, the breaking of a twig as some animal landed upon it.

Tarik sat all that day, and the next as well, but heard nothing. And then, on the third day, there came to him not so much a sound as a presence. It was not distinct, but it was there.

There was the song of a bird. There were the scurrying feet of some tiny creature.

The presence again. Rhythmically.

The sound of his own leg against the ground as he shifted position. The sound of the wind stirring the tree-tops.

The presence again. Now, more than a presence, it sounded like the distant sounding of Atumpan drums.

There were scratching sounds made by a squirrel as he climbed halfway up a tree.

Atumpan drums of his heart sounded quietly, one beat soft, the other yet softer.

A bird called from beyond the gardens and then was answered.

Pa-Tump. Pa-Tump. Pa-Tump. The sound of his own heart beat in Tarik's ears like a memory of something long forgotten.

31

Pa-Tump. Pa-Tump. Pa-Tump. Tarik heard the sound of his own heart beating with a fragility that dared him to breathe.

But he had heard it.

"Shall I tell you a story today?" asked Nongo the following morning.

"Do you have one, friend?" asked Tarik.

"Yes." Nongo smiled. "I have one."

"Is it about a blind man who is robbed of his purse?"

"Ah, you know it!" Nongo said, smiling. "And what now have you learned from it?"

"I have thought about it all night," Tarik said. "But I have learned nothing more than I have told you."

"Little brother," Nongo said patiently, "you are beginning to learn to use the things that are given you. You begin to see, you begin even to hear. For some men this is enough. But only to see and only to hear is like being half a man. You must learn to feel as well."

"But if the blind man could not see the robbers, if he could not hear them, how would he catch them so that he could feel them?" Tarik asked.

"With the spirit that all men possess," Nongo said, "it is possible to reach out to all other things. Put your gaze upon the ground before you. Do you see the sun?"

"I do."

"Reach your hands up toward the sun, without moving your eyes."

Tarik reached high and to his left. When he had done

this, Nongo asked him if the sun was truly where he had reached.

"Yes," Tarik replied. "I could feel its warmth against my skin."

"The warmth of the sun is its spirit," Nongo said. "All things, large and small, have spirits such as these. Again, do not move your eyes. There is a rock in this garden. It is large and gray. Can you feel it?"

"I cannot," said Tarik.

"You can," Nongo replied, "if you will."

Nongo spread both hands in front of himself, palms outward, and spread them in a wide circle.

"Close your eyes if it helps," Nongo said.

Tarik did this and again brought his arms around in a wide circle. For a moment he thought he felt something, but he was not sure. Again and again he reached out, trying to feel where the rock was. He could feel the sun easily enough, and the slight breeze, but that was all.

Finally he thought he felt something. He moved his arms away and brought them slowly around again. There he was sure that he felt something. He opened his eyes and looked up. No more than ten feet in front of him was the strangest creature he had ever seen! A heavily swaddled figure with dark eyes that stared fiercely into his own. It was a person, its face half covered with a makeshift veil, who stood before him. He could feel and hear his heart beat faster. Then, as suddenly as it appeared, the figure whirled and went away. Tarik turned quickly to Nongo.

"What was that?"

"There is no need for you to know that now," said
Nongo. "There are other things that you must learn. You
cannot fill your head with mysteries or they will bind you
forever. You will know in time. Know now that you felt
her presence when she neared you. That, too, is really a
beginning."

Tarik knew he would learn nothing more about the
strange person until Nongo was ready.

"Do you feel things as well?" Tarik asked, returning to
their conversation.

"As well as a man who has no light to pull his attention
elsewhere," Nongo answered.

Tarik looked into the face of Nongo and saw that it was
calm. He waited for him to speak again, but Nongo sat
quietly. It was then that Tarik slowly raised his hand and
stopped it just before Nongo's face. He was about to ask
Nongo if he felt the presence of his hand when a smile
came to Nongo's face and Tarik started to withdraw his
hand, thinking that Nongo was going to speak. Nongo
did not speak, but caught Tarik's fingers as he moved
them away. He held them in his own hand for a moment,
then patted them with his other hand before he let them
go.

"Do you smile, little brother?" Nongo asked.

"I smile," Tarik answered.

"It is good," Nongo said.

"Where do you come from?" Tarik asked. "How is it
you are in such a place as this when your face is so much
like what I see when I look at myself in the water?"

"I am from that place in Alkebu-lan that has a river

much the same as yours," Nongo said. "My people were workers of iron, my father and his father before him. I was given to the tasks of the spirit and of the mind as a young man. I have studied with the wise men of many lands, both in my home of Meroe and away from that lovely place.

"When I had drunk of knowledge, I thought that I would quickly quench my thirst, but it was not to be. So I traveled and studied much, returning home each five years to teach among my people and to learn there also. This I have been doing for so many years that they seem beyond counting."

"I think you know everything now," Tarik said.

"No, that is not so," Nongo said. "When I reached the prime of my years, I gave up seeking the science of man in order to know his essence. I thought that would be a good thing and within my grasp, for I had already studied much. But then a wondrous thing happened to me. I found that what I had seen with the eyes of a young man changed shapes and colors as my eyes grew older. And what I had only smelled as a young man I was able to taste as life fell behind me.

"When I came to this land, El Muerte was not much older than you are now. Even as a youth he made men pay him the homage he felt his due. Those who did not suffered his anger. But where men had failed in their challenge of strength against strength, I thought that I would prevail with wisdom. My moment came, and I found that I did not know the meaning of strength or the uses of wisdom. But even what is lost to me may guide another's footsteps, little brother. Docao and I found each other groping along the same path one day and decided to walk together. So here I am at this place."

"And here am I," Tarik said.

He held up his hand, and again Nongo took it in his own.

FOUR

SHE WAS LIKE A DREAM, SOMETHING THAT EXISTED only in the shadows of the mind or in the flash of sunlight upon the water. He had seen her, or parts of her, in the Gardens of Shange. There would be a movement, a fleeting shadow, and she would disappear.

Once Tarik had seen her up close. He had been awakened by the coolness of the wind against his face in the early morning. When he sat up, he had seen her standing, stark still, outside his window. He was startled at first, and then it came to him that it was she, the strange creature who existed in an almost secret fashion in the Gardens of Shange. She stood looking into his open window, and the thought came to Tarik that it was she who had opened the shutters, and not the wind.

Her face was not remarkable, except for her eyes. They were dark and seemed to draw him in. It was as if she could not see, but bade her eyes draw in what she would know about, which they did.

"Good day to you!" Tarik raised his voice to her.

There was no answer, but she did not move from the place where she stood. He stood and went to the window and looked out at her. She was thin and vined about herself like a small tree in the forest hidden from the sun. In the gray light of dawn he could see that her face was the color of sand or nearly so. She was dressed simply in the way of desert traders. Tarik imagined her to be from this land in which he found himself.

"Do you speak?" he asked of her.

She did not answer but stood motionless, almost as if she were not a real person, but some thing—a tree, a rock, an image of a person. Then she moved away, seemingly without haste, and was gone so quickly that it was almost as if she had not been there.

"Who is the girl?" Tarik asked Docao the next day. Docao that day was teaching him to use the dagger.

"Now, hold the handle of the dagger toward the tree," Docao said, ignoring his question. "Then turn the wrist as you bring the dagger across your body so that the full force of your weight and strength is behind the blade as it strikes."

"You have not answered my question about the girl," Tarik said.

"You must remember that it is the cutting edge that you must strike with and not the point. The point is for lovers to prick their skins and mingle small droplets of blood."

Tarik cocked his wrist so that the blade of the dagger he had been given rested against his wrist. Then he stepped forward quickly, as he had been told to do, thrusting the knife as straight toward the tree as he could while twisting his wrist so that the full cutting edge struck at the same time.

"That was quite good, really," Docao said. "Quite good."

"Is she a secret?" Tarik persisted.

"A secret?" Docao rubbed his side with an elbow. "Why do you ask?"

"I see her movements about this place and yet I do not know either her name or her mission here," Tarik said. "I do not see her attending to our needs, and yet she is a girl."

"Attending to our needs, indeed," Docao chuckled. "Here, sit beside me."

Docao sat on the still-damp grass and leaned against a tree. Tarik sat opposite him, leaning back on one elbow so that he could see the expressions on the old man's pale face as he spoke.

"When you first came here, we asked you to do many things, Tarik," Docao said. "One of the things we asked you to do was to control your hate for El Muerte, who killed your father. You were not the first to suffer losses at this evil man's hands, and I am sure he has already seen to it that your losses have not been the last.

"The girl came to us first," Docao continued. "She had also seen her people die. She had been wandering for weeks almost without eating, and scarcely sleeping. She was ill-used and in poor condition when one of the farmers in a nearby village found her, took pity on her, and brought her here. The hate that she had for El Muerte was what gave us the idea of training a young person to do what must be done."

"A girl?" Tarik asked with a laugh. "To do a man's task?"

"Yes," Docoa answered, "a girl. And if you fail we might yet look to her. But she is a strange one. She is like a guitar that one strums seeking the soothing sounds of a sweet tune but that responds only with the most violent discord. Perhaps, one day, if she can control those storms within her bosom . . .

"Her people had lived in these parts for many years," Docao continued. "They were the kind of people that become part of the land, that invest their blood and their children in the soil. When El Muerte's men destroyed her family, she ran away, not from fear—as they imagined—but rather possessed with a certain kind of madness from which she has not yet fully recovered, and from which she may never recover."

"Still, a man's task is a man's task," Tarik said. "It is the use of a bowl to hold water."

"Do you believe that?" Docao asked.

"It is nothing to believe or to disbelieve," Tarik answered. "It is simply so."

"Then perhaps you can train today with Stria."

"Stria?" Tarik asked. "Is that her name?"

"The best that we can make out," Docao said, standing. "You wait here and I will ask Nongo if it is all right. It will be amusing."

When Docao had gone, Tarik closed his eyes and let the sun warm his face. Soon he would be ready to seek out and kill El Muerte, he knew. When that was done, he would make the long journey to the land of his people and tell them all that had happened. For the first time in months he thought of his father. He remembered how his father had looked as death approached, how he could have been praying as he lifted his arm to the skies to ward off the blows. But it was not to heaven that he had lifted his arm in the last terrible moment, but to the steel of his assassin.

"Tarik." Docao stood suddenly above him. "Are you ready?"

Tarik shielded his eyes from the sun. Nongo stood some distance behind Docao with the girl. They had put a garment on her that covered her from her shoulders to her knees. It looked like the hide of a camel. In her hands she held a sword that was two-thirds her height and that she held in both hands.

"She has learned to use the weapons," Docao said. "As you will see."

Docao gave Tarik a sword, one that he had not seen before. Tarik touched the blade with his thumb and saw that it had not been sharpened and considered this just as well, for he did not wish to injure the girl.

Both Nongo and Docao backed away and left Tarik and the girl Stria in the center of the gardens. Tarik took several steps toward Stria, allowing his sword to point only at her feet as he approached her. Docao had not told him how they would practice together, only that they would.

Tarik was thinking of what he would do, when suddenly she began to scream. Stria's screams stopped Tarik. She held the sword in her extended arms, the tip of it describing a circle, the sun sliding along its broad edge. Then she was moving faster toward him and with a fury. The screaming began again and then stopped as she stopped only a few feet from him. She turned away, or seemed to, and then was facing him again, the black eyes reaching for him even as the sword whistled through the air.

It was all he could do to fall on one knee and bring his own weapon up quickly enough to stop the blow mere inches from his face. Stria swung the sword above her head, started it down in one direction toward his head, and then twisted it toward his ribs. Tarik dove away from her, pushing his sword in front of his exposed ribs. He felt his weapon being taken from his hand with the force of her blow and saw it fly high into the midmorning sun.

He bounced to his feet and threw himself to the spot where the sword would come down. As he turned to see where Stria was, he reached blindly for his sword. Stria had not moved from where she stood. Tarik found the sword and stood, breathing deeply as he did so. Stria moved toward him again, twisting the sword menacingly before her.

This time he prepared himself for her charge and matched it with his own. He brought his sword hard against the base of hers. The sparks showered about them crazily, but she did not drop her sword. She took a step backward and then came at him again with all of the ferocity of the first charge. He warded off first one blow and then another and then what seemed to be an endless stream as she stood before him. And so quick were her blows that he hardly had time to strike any of his own.

It was clear that this was not a game to Stria. Tarik began to parry harder and harder, turning his wrist into his movements so that he could drive her sword farther from her body with each blow, as he had been taught. But he did not succeed. Finally it was Docao and Nongo who ended the match. Docao took Stria away, his arm around her, her body still shaking from her efforts.

"She would not surrender," Nongo said to Tarik. "To conquer her you would have to kill her. But she has turned so much into herself that she cannot conquer her own rage. I think perhaps she will one day."

"I am surprised that she is so strong," Tarik said.

"Do not be!" There was a harshness in Nongo's voice that surprised Tarik. "The body is only as strong as the mind is willing. If you do not know this, you will never survive against an enemy who seeks your destruction."

Tarik sat on the ground. His breathing was still heavy, and perspiration beaded his lips. The sun was high, and birds which had earlier chittered gaily along the tops of the trees seeking the most succulent buds now rested in the bottom branches away from the heat of midday. After a while Docao returned to the gardens and began to pick the fruit from a cherry tree, cupping a sack over the stump of his right arm in which to drop them.

Stria appeared again. She stood in the shade along the house, looking at Tarik. Then she moved slowly along the wall and disappeared in the shadows.

FIVE

TARIK GREW WEARY OF THE DAYS OF ENDLESS TRAIN-
ing and eager to be about the task he had set for himself. Each day the tasks set for him by Docao and Nongo
became less demanding. His arms grew strong and his
senses keen, but each time he asked if it was time for him to
begin his quest for El Muerte, they bade him have patience
for yet another day. And so it continued in this manner
for many months, long past the time that Tarik found
interest in the exercises devised for him. Then, one bright
morning, just as he thought that his mentors had forgotten the purpose they had assigned him, Tarik was summoned by Nongo and found him sitting cross-legged in
the shade of a tree.

"Once"—Nongo began speaking even before Tarik had
settled himself on the ground—"there was a brown sparrow that lived a good life. He sang his songs each day to
the Spirit that created him and neither thought nor com-
mitted evil. The sparrow came to know, by what was said
of him, and by what he saw in the part of the world in

which he lived, that he was indeed a creature free of blemish.

"There lived, too, in this same part of the world, a snake. And where the sparrow was pure in his life, so the snake was evil. This snake paid homage to nothing but himself. He delighted in the fear he struck in the hearts of those around him, and reveled in their misfortunes.

"When these two, the sparrow and the snake, by chance encountered each other, the snake immediately pounced on the sparrow. The sparrow, of course, demanded that he be released at once. He argued that he was a good bird, thinking in his heart that he approached the state of being perfect in his goodness, although he would not make such a claim aloud. He argued, too, that his song was of great beauty and brought much pleasure to the world. All these things were true. Then the evil snake, having heard these arguments and knowing that they were true, devoured the sparrow, caring neither for his goodness nor his song."

Then Nongo ceased speaking and rubbed his hands together as he waited for Tarik's reply.

"I am not a sparrow," Tarik said. "The sparrow was helpless against the snake."

"We may well match the strength of men, Tarik," Nongo said, "but some men have another strength, born of the evil they serve, that cannot be matched by steel or flesh. Such men can strike without the weight of remorse on their arm, they can kill without the glare of either reason or mercy to misdirect the blow. To such men we are all sparrows."

"Why do you tell me these things?" Tarik got up and moved away from Nongo.

"Only so that your pride will not close your eyes to the ways of the world, my son," Nongo replied. "Many before you have fallen in the names of their gods, and many have perished in their sleep not knowing that evil never slumbers. But I have not brought you this far to turn you away. There are powers in this world, powers that lie between the light of day and the black of night, between the cry and the sound, that are little dreamed of and less known. These, if you have the courage, can be yours."

"Are they powers of evil or of good?" Tarik asked.

"They can become powers of evil if you serve them," Nongo replied, "but they will serve the good man and neither tarnish him nor make him less than he was. Yet their very power holds danger for us as well. We become like the pool that invites the ocean to its bosom, hoping to surrender less than will be gained."

"I am not afraid," Tarik said.

He fell on his knees before Nongo and took his hands in his own. "Tell me of these things."

"There are three things that will be of good use to you," Nongo continued. "The first is a sword. It is called the Sword of Serq. It is guarded by a specter, the sister of Evil itself. Every man who has sought to grasp this sword has failed. But it is a wondrous sword, for once in hand it cannot be broken, nor will it fall from the hand."

"Then I must have it!" Tarik said.

"There is a valley," Nongo said, "less than two days'

47

journey from here. In the valley there is a dense wood in which the wind never ceases to howl and where the sun never shines. In the center of the wood is the hut of the specter. On the wall of the hut the sword is mounted on a great shield. Take the sword but do not touch the shield. The specter will be sleeping in the hut—it may take any shape.

"Once you have touched the sword, the specter will awake. When it does, you must not look away from its face until you have left the wood. As long as you do not turn away, it cannot harm you. It is powerful only when you turn away from it, and if that happens, it will surely destroy you. Do you understand this?"

"Do not worry, old man," Tarik said. "I will not flinch so easily."

"Tell me," Nongo said calmly. "When your father was killed, did you not turn away?"

Tarik did not answer, for he knew he had.

"Do not be ashamed," Nongo said. "We must often sift our weaknesses to find our strengths."

Tarik started out early the next day. Before leaving, he had spoken again with Nongo, who repeated the warning to him. He spent a few moments alone with his thoughts, summoning the strength of his spirit for the journey. Just before he left he saw the girl, standing silently in a corner of the gardens. He lifted his hand to her, but she did not respond.

The journey was more difficult than Tarik had imagined it would be. He went through the mountains, following the small map that Docao had drawn for him, and forded a wide but shallow stream that twisted its way through the range of white mountains. Nongo had told him to arrive before night fell on the second day, and it was all he could do to keep up. He passed a few small farms and some shepherds tending their flocks but walked away from them, heeding what Nongo had said—that words often betrayed the lips that spoke them.

On the second day he reached the two mountains that guarded the valley. In his mind's eye he saw himself walking quickly through the wood, seizing the sword and leaving without great difficulty. But when he had actually reached the wood, the coolness of the wind shocked him and he knew that it would be no easy task. Nevertheless he took a deep breath and entered the foreboding tangle of trees and vines.

The chilled wind whipped about his legs and sent leaves and branches into his face. When he had taken only a few steps into the wood, he turned to look back and saw that already it was impossible to see out of it. It was as if a curtain of darkness had been drawn around the place and around him as well. He pressed on, cautiously guiding each step deeper and deeper through the darkness. The howling of the wind grew louder and louder, and Tarik followed the sound until he saw, finally, the outline of the hut before him.

It was smaller than he had thought it would be, and irregular in shape. Its roof was pitched slightly and was partially obscured by an overhanging branch. There were no windows that Tarik could see. Neither was there a door, but there was an opening in the corner of the strange dwelling, and it was through this that Tarik, bending slightly, entered. A candle on the table, unaffected by the wind that swirled around the room, afforded a dim light by which Tarik could see fairly well. On a pallet on the floor a woman slept. Ordinary in appearance except for the length of her hair, which reached her ankles, she breathed deeply in her slumber but did not otherwise stir. As Tarik watched her breathe, he understood that it was her breath that was the wind in the wood. He shuddered slightly and began to look for the sword. He found it on the wall opposite the woman. It was on the shield, as Nongo had said. The handle was ivory, circled with gold that wound its way to the end and then formed the shape of a scorpion. Tarik, careful not to touch the shield, took the sword down from the wall.

The roar startled him. He jumped back and saw the tiger on the pallet. He was not sure whether this beast was the person he had seen lying a moment before on the floor, but he remembered Nongo's warning not to take his eyes from those of the creature. The beast crouched low, its tail twitching above its body. Then it leaped toward him with a single move. Tarik moved back quickly, but he did not take his eyes from those of the tiger, which stopped inches before him.

Then, as quickly as it had become a tiger, the specter changed into a man with the face of a rat. It stood snarling so close to Tarik that if he had moved his face the length of his nose he would have touched it. Tarik backed out of the house as quickly as he could, holding the sword in front of him with one hand, trying to feel his way with the other.

Once out of the hut, the man changed to a boar, grunting at Tarik's feet, its eyes dark and beady and fixed on his face. The boar sniffed and rooted at Tarik's feet but did not touch him. Still, Tarik backed slowly through the wood, not really sure of his direction.

The boar faded away and in its place grew the lovely form of a girl.

"There"—she smiled, and lifted her arms to Tarik— "you have gained the sword. Take me with you also, and I will serve you as well as the sword. You must only close your eyes and kiss me to seal the bargain."

Tarik did not speak, nor did he close his eyes, but continued to back away from the creature before him.

"My son! My son! Turn away from this pain I suffer."

Now it was Ntah, Tarik's father, his bloodstained hand before his face, an anguished eye peering from between the gnarled black fingers. "Do not look at me like this, my son."

Tarik could feel the tears stinging his eyes as he backed away from the image of his father.

"Be away from me, evil thing," Tarik cried.

The instant he spoke, there appeared before him a giant, nearly twice his size. The sweat was pouring from its face, and its bloodshot eyes blinked furiously.

Tarik could feel neither his arms nor his legs as he backed away. His mouth was dry as he gasped for breath, and he wanted nothing more than to rid himself of the horrible thing before him. He found himself both wanting to believe the creature before him and terrified of the consequences of heeding it.

The giant roared strange words at Tarik, words that he did not understand but that made his skin crawl. The giant leaned closer to him, so that he could feel its breath against his cheek. The giant was whispering, but the whisper came to Tarik like the rushing of the sea in his ears.

"You will never leave here alive," the giant roar-whispered. "The old ones have fooled you. You will walk backwards until your legs grow as weak as the blades of grass beneath your feet, and then it is I who will pounce upon you and strike you dead! Your legs grow weary. Your arms grow weary. Drop the blade and run for your life while you still have life in your black form! Your eyes grow weary. Look upon my face and see your death! *Look upon my face and see your death!*"

And Tarik looked deeply into the giant's eyes and saw himself lying on a patch of arid ground covered with his own blood, buzzards on his chest and limbs, eating his flesh as he lay dying. But still he did not turn away, and at the edge of the wood the giant screamed and turned into an asp, and then into a gorgon and into the form of a man with horns and a thick tongue that hung limply from its mouth, and even as Tarik moved from the wood the last thing he saw of the specter was the fiercely smoldering hatred in its evil eyes.

Then Tarik started back toward the Gardens of Shange.

On the way he met two thieves who plied their wicked trade along the highway.

"Little brother," one of them called to him. "Where does such a slight black lad get such a fine-looking sheath as that? And does the sword it contains resemble it in fineness?"

Tarik did not reply but started to walk in a large circle around them. They watched him, amused. Then, quickly, one of them sprang to his feet and pulled a dagger from his garment. He went to one side of Tarik while the other thief stood his ground. Tarik saw him also reach into his garment and saw him produce a sling, the kind that shepherds use to chase wolves.

"If you put down your possessions I will not kill you," the one with the sling sneered. His teeth were large and yellowed from chewing bark.

"Leave me in peace," Tarik answered.

"Pieces is more like it!" The one with the dagger stepped forward just as the other one unloosed a large staff toward Tarik.

Instinctively Tarik brought the sword up, just in time to stop the flight of the hurled staff.

"*Serq!*"

The thief with the sling screamed the name of the sword.

"It is the Sword of Serq!"

With this cry both thieves ran off as quickly as they could. Tarik wondered how they knew what sword it was. Then he looked down at the staff that had been hurled at him and saw that the sword had cut it in two. It was indeed a wondrous sword.

When Tarik reached the gardens and had told Nongo all that had transpired, Nongo said that he had done well. Still, there was a strange look about the old man that worried Tarik.

"What is it that your mind sees?" Tarik asked him.

"Things went well in the wood," Nongo answered. "I have offered many prayers for your safe return and praise the heavens that I hear your voice again. But your encounter with the thieves is not a good omen."

"Bah." Tarik spat on the ground. "I beat them off easily."

"They know about the sword," Nongo said. He extended his hand over the table until he could feel the heat of the candle, and lifted it.

"If they know about the sword, they will know that you are no ordinary person they encountered. Even the smallest candle brightens a dark night."

"But are they privy to El Muerte's table?" asked Tarik.

"Evil has a way of finding evil," Nongo said. "You must rest tonight and begin your next quest in the morning."

"So soon?"

"It is not soon enough, I fear," Nongo said, "but I pray that it will do."

When Nongo had left him, Tarik felt disappointed. For instead of making much over his accomplishment, Nongo seemed worried. Tarik took Serq to his room and leaned it against the rough wall so he could look at it from his bed. Tarik looked at the sword for a long time just as it was, and then he took a candle and placed it behind Serq so that the light seemed to run along its edges and make of it a thing of great beauty. He felt swollen with pride at what he had done.

As he gazed at Serq, the candle grew less bright until it was little more than a soft glow behind the great sword. Tarik closed his eyes and tried to imagine himself in the same hard circle in which his father had died. He saw himself standing tall and brave as El Muerte rushed at him. Again and again he pictured how he would use Serq to fend off every blow that El Muerte offered, until at last his foe knelt before him begging for his miserable life.

Tarik's eyes opened to complete darkness. The room was suddenly cool, and the trickle of perspiration that ran down his side made him shiver. He lay in the dark, eyes wide open, as a memory of a time long ago came to him. He was nine, and his father had made him a short spear. The blade had not been made of bone, as were the ones of his friends, but from a piece of dark, flat iron that his father had got from a traveler. His father had sharpened it and attached it to a thin ebony shaft and had fixed red, green, and black feathers to its tail so that it would throw true. Tarik remembered his father had given him the spear and told him to guard their home while he was away gathering shrubs to make gold dyes.

Tarik had told his mother that he was going to kill all the warriors in the village and become king of all the Songhai people, and then he would kill the warriors of the

Hausa people and become their king as well. He had followed her around, telling her these things, and finally she had brought a hen to him and tied its leg to a small branch and told him to kill it for their supper. He had walked away from the hen and thrown the spear, but could not hit it. He told her that he couldn't hit the hen, and she made him come closer. He had cried when he saw the blood and the awful flapping the hen had made. He had cried, and still she had made him kill the hen. When he had finally succeeded in killing the hen, he had gone to his mother and put his arms around her stout legs, but she had pushed him away and told him that when he learned to kill he could no longer be a child.

Now, in the cold darkness of his room, he thought of this and tried to imagine himself striking down El Muerte. He wondered if, when the moment came, he would be able to do such a thing.

SIX

THAT NIGHT TARIK DREAMED OF A BARELY REMEM-
bered land far away. He was sitting with his friends
Omoyuri and Emeka at the foot of a large storehouse,
where kola nuts and yami were stored, while they told
stories and watched distant clouds change from fluffy white
camels to thin cotton wisps in the scorched sky. When
Tarik awoke, it was at the urging of Docao, who was pre-
paring breakfast.

"Good morning." Docao spoke cheerfully. "I trust you
have rested well?"

"I have," Tarik replied, not bothering to cover the yawn
that muffled his words, "but I think I could have rested
longer."

"Man dwells upon the earth such a short time," Docao
said, throwing open the window so that the cool morning
breeze could fill the room, "and yet he would spend so
much of it resting. I wonder whatever for?"

In the middle of the table was a brown earthen bowl
filled with thin strips of lamb, white raisins, and slivers of

onion. Tarik watched as Docao heated a large shallow pan that hung in the brick fireplace. When the pan was hot, he poured onto it a thick liquid and quickly followed it with the mixture of lamb, raisins, and onions. This he stirred until the meat sizzled noisily and filled the room with a sweet pungency. Then he took a flask of wine and sprinkled it liberally on the mixture until the hissing stopped.

"Nongo has told me that you did well in getting the sword," Docao said, still slowly stirring the hearty breakfast. "You are to be congratulated."

"It was nothing," Tarik said.

"Nothing indeed!" Docao replied. The mixture had begun to cook loudly again, and Docao stirred it more rapidly. Then he took a copper ladle and scooped a goodly portion into Tarik's bowl.

"Men have tried before, but were failed by either their skills or their nerve. You seem to have an ample supply of both."

"Will Nongo tell me what I have to do today?" Tarik asked. He picked up a tender morsel of lamb with the tip of his knife and placed it in his mouth.

"No," Docao said. "That task is up to me. Nongo goes to the shadows today."

"What is that place?" Tarik asked.

"The shadows?" Docao looked at Tarik and then turned away. "It is not so much a place as it is a state of mind, I suppose. Nongo goes within himself to seek the courage that he must have to live on. He is a great man, and powerful, too.

"But let us not dwell on him today. It is you we must work with," Docao said. "Today you must seek the Crystal of Truth. To call it the Crystal of the Heart's Truth would be more precise, for that is what it truly is, and it is as remarkable a thing as I have known about. It is in a shallow lake, no more than a day's journey from this place. If you do not waste time, you will reach it sometime during the night."

"What does this Crystal do?" Tarik asked. "It does not sound like a weapon."

"Not sound like a weapon? There are those who would dispute that, but never mind. It allows one to see truth without the curving glance of experience. Only this and nothing more," Docao said. "It will not allow the mind to see what it will not comprehend, nor will it tell what is to be. But it will remove what one *wants* to see, and what is twisted by hope or anguish, and reveal what is truly in the heart."

"Then why do I need it?" Tarik asked. "It is said among my people that there is nothing but truth in a stone because it is so simple. Is it not a simple thing that I have to do—to avenge the death of my father?"

Docao turned to Tarik and watched as the young man took a piece of bread and ran it along the bottom of his bowl to get the last of the sauce.

"Truth is simple only for the young, my friend," Docao said. "You will discover one day that there are as many truths as there are eyes. Each of us seeks his own, and few of us will see that of another. I pray you trust me in this matter, and Nongo as well. Our lives lie in those skins we have long ago shed on paths that you will perhaps never see. What we bring is ourselves only, stripped of all the usual ambitions that would distort our vision. As much as you can, trust us. We will not betray you."

"Is there a specter guarding this Crystal?" Tarik asked.

"No," Docao answered. "The Crystal is in the middle of a small lake, as I said. At night it can be seen glowing. One has only to wade into the water and take it up. But it is guarded by a great beast that is half human, half monster. It has but one eye, and that it keeps fixed on the Crystal. Sometimes it tires and closes the eye, and only then is it safe to attempt to capture its prize."

"It sounds too easy," Tarik said. "Why has no one taken this Crystal before?"

"Well, why indeed?" Docao sat and looked toward the heavens, rubbing his neck with the end of his stump.

"Perhaps it is because there are so few young people like yourself who either know about the Crystal or have the skills and courage to attempt to get it. Or perhaps because we are all filled with illusions of sense and time, and as we grow older we begin to realize that only truth can destroy those illusions. Truth becomes a more formidable opponent than death ever was."

"I don't understand all these things you say, Docao."

"Which proves the mercy of the Lord," Docao replied. "But now that you have celebrated your stomach in such a hearty fashion, you must be off. I've again drawn one of my little maps for you. There is a mare that you can ride, but don't abuse her. On the map you will find a road down which you will travel, keeping the sun over your

right shoulder until it sinks. In due time you will come to
a place where the trees touch branches over the road. There
you will find another path, large enough for one person to
pass at a time. This path will lead you to the lake. Go in
peace, and with God."

Docao stood and started to leave, but Tarik took him
by the wrist.

"Docao," he said earnestly, "how is it that you and
Nongo know these things?"

"We were both men who believed in ourselves and our
gods at one time, my son," Docao answered. "Now that
we understand how frail we are, we have begun to open
our hearts to other things—perhaps best left alone. We
know the price we must pay."

And with those words Docao left the room.

Tarik sat still for a long moment, reflecting upon what
Docao had said, until his thoughts were interrupted by the
girl, who brought him a flask of water and a piece of fruit
to take along on his journey.

"I bring you these things as a gift," Stria said. "Tell me
of the thing you wear around your neck."

"This?" Tarik touched the amulet he wore. "It is a
small thing my father fashioned for me."

Stria loosened her belt and took from it a small bracelet
of hair that had been braided around strands of fine silver.

"This is all I have to touch of my mother," she said.
"Take it, and give me what you are wearing."

"I cannot," Tarik said. "It is too dear to me. I am
sorry."

The girl looked at the bracelet in her hands and then at

Tarik. Tarik saw there were tears in her eyes. She brought the bracelet to her bosom, held it there briefly, and then put it in his hand and closed his fingers over it. Tarik looked at her, and she did not look away. Even when he had taken the fruit and water from her and had ridden through the arched door, he felt the weight of her eyes upon him.

Tarik traveled in the direction that Docao had told him about, always keeping the sun over his right shoulder as he did so. It was a good day; the sky was clear and pleasant, and the green fields stretched before him like an emerald sea undulating softly through the rolling hills. By his side hung the sword, Serq, and its being there was a great comfort to him as he journeyed. He did not stop to rest. He ate the fruit when the sun had reached its highest point, and drank sparingly of the water the girl had given him. He found himself thinking much about her, wondering how such fury could lie crouching behind the dark calmness of her eyes.

As the sun began to sink, he grew weary and stopped to rest beneath a stand of silver-leaved olive trees. Then he pushed on, searching for the place that Docao had spoken of. In the distance he saw it, a place where the trees touched over the road. Tarik found the path and headed down it. The sun set soon after, and the countryside fell into darkness and was filled with the sounds of night.

Crickets whistled softly, and crawling things scampered on the ground. He peered into the darkness, at that place

where he thought he had seen the sun's rays on the
ground, and saw a tiny sliver of light. As he drew nearer
he saw that it was indeed the lake that he was seeking. He
came as close as he dared on his horse, then dismounted
and knelt on one knee in the bushes. The moon was not
yet visible, and it was difficult for Tarik to see.

He listened to the sound of his heart beating and
thought that surely all the world must hear as well, for it
was pounding madly. His fingers stroked the handle of
Serq, and more than once he withdrew it partially from
his scabbard, only to replace it again.

The place was not cold, as had been the woods. There
were some trees: lemon trees that twisted oddly in the
night, and a few large oaks, but that was all. Tarik swept
his eyes across the dimness time and time again, trying to
see more than he did, but to little avail. Then he thought
he saw something. It was a light ahead of him. He
crouched even lower in the bush where he had been kneeling and stared intently. Soon there was no mistaking it;
there was a glow coming from the middle of the lake. He
had found the Crystal.

He saw nothing around him, and his first impulse was
to move at once to the lake and seize the Crystal. He
would keep one hand always on his sword, so if the beast
did appear he would dispatch him quickly. But he waited
a while longer, remembering Docao's words and wondering if the moon would ever rise that night.

As Tarik pondered these things, he shifted his position
slightly to relieve the aching in his legs from the long

ride and the cramped position he had assumed. As he thought of these things, his nostrils were suddenly assailed by an odor so foul, so putrid, that it nearly turned his stomach. He caught his breath sharply and turned to see, less than three arm spans away from him, the beast of the lake!

It did not crawl so much as it dragged itself along the ground, writhing and snarling as it did so, its one eye rolling about loosely in its socket, from which oozed a liquid that poured down over its quivering mouth.

Tarik did not move as it slithered by him on the edge of the lake. It was nearly twice the length of a man's body and seemed to be, in some aspects, a human creature. Except for the one wildly rolling eye, the nose, sharp, almost beak-like, and the gaping, quivering mouth could have been human features. They were hideous, but not so far from human that upon viewing the creature the nightmare of its possible humanity would not come to mind. Its body was covered with scales from its almost man-like shoulders to its webbed appendages by which it dragged itself laboriously along the ground.

Tarik wiped his mouth and noticed that his hands were sweating. Even after the beast had passed, its smell lingered behind it, and it wasn't until it had gone nearly to the other side of the lake—a fact that Tarik could now make out as the moon made its appearance through the heavy clouds—that the odor subsided.

There was something else on the other side of the lake as well. Tarik saw a furry animal come to the edge of the lake to drink. It could have been a fox or something smaller. Just as Tarik saw it, the creature saw it as well and increased its speed beyond anything Tarik would have thought possible.

The fox stood frozen in the moonlight for a long moment before the beast hurled itself through the air at it. The fox started to scamper away, but a second too late. The beast of the lake had landed next to it and now had sunk its fangs into the furry side of the fox. The fox yelped and nipped furiously at the beast, but to no avail. The beast of the lake did not move, except for the swelling and contracting of its glistening torso. The furry animal flopped madly, and then, as if its blood were being drained by the creature, it became smaller, and smaller, until with one final quiver it lay small and dead in the low marshes.

The creature stirred, shaking its head from one side to the other. Tarik watched it, not realizing for a while that it had resumed its same movement, dragging itself about the edges of the lake.

Tarik had hoped that when the moon rose to its highest point the beast would be on the other side of the lake, but that was not to be. The beast stretched slowly, almost painfully toward the moon as the light whitened the surface of the lake. Then the beast sank slowly back to earth and blinked its one great eye, still rolling it about as it did so, until it was finally closed. Still, the beast did not lie down, but sat upright, motionless, and Tarik knew that in this position it must be asleep.

Tarik ran his hand along the hilt of his sword and then

rose from where he was kneeling. He went quickly toward the lake, making little noise. The water was cold but refreshing.

As quietly as he could he waded toward where the Crystal lay beneath the surface of the water. When he reached it, he put his hand into the water and grasped it. It was warm, even though it lay a full sword's length beneath the water. When Tarik brought it out of the water, it ceased to shine. He wrapped it quickly in the cloth he had brought with him and tied it to his belt. Then he began to wade out of the lake, away from where the beast slept. He had almost reached the far shore when the beast stirred. Tarik started to race for the shore, his legs splashing wildly through the water. He slipped but regained his footing quickly as he pulled himself up onto the muddy banks. There was a splashing in the water, and Tarik turned to see the beast swimming furiously toward him. In the water it moved even faster than it did on land, and Tarik found himself backing away in dread fascination as the beast closed the distance between them.

Tarik raced through the marshes, tearing his legs in some of the larger thickets as he ran. It was the smell of the beast that overcame him first. He could smell it gaining on him, and then he heard the peculiar gurgling noise it seemed to make.

Tarik saw that the bushes around the lake were too dense for him to run through except for the small area in which he had been earlier concealed. He had to reach that point or fight the beast. When he looked toward the side of the lake from which he had come and saw how far away it was, he knew he had no choice. He drew his sword, even as he ran, and then stopped to face the onrushing beast.

It did not hesitate, but flung itself through the air, even as it had when it had attacked the fox. Again it landed, not on its intended victim, but within an arm's length of Tarik.

Tarik swung the sword between where he stood and the beast's hideous head. The beast stopped its charge, lifting itself to Tarik's height, hissing and gurgling. Tarik lashed out at the beast again, striking it in the side. The sword hit cleanly, but there was neither blood from the wound nor respite from the beast's fury. The beast struck again, knocking Tarik to one knee. Tarik moved the sword just in front of its striking mouth, the fangs clanging noisily against the iron of his blade. Tarik backed away, hacking fruitlessly at the wildly flopping creature. Wherever he hit, the blade would strike true but the beast would come on, forcing Tarik back inch by inch until finally Tarik felt the coldness of the water at his back. He tried to move back toward the land, but the beast cut him off at every turn. The beast's fangs struck again and again, first at Tarik's throat, then at the sword. Tarik's arms ached with the effort of repulsing the horrid creature. Now his foot was in the water. He realized that once in the water he could not swing the sword and would be at the mercy of the beast. Now frigid waters numbed his aching knees as he still was being forced back.

The beast grabbed the blade of the sword with the gaping, snarling orifice it used as a mouth, fastening its fangs around it and twisting its head until Tarik thought that it would pull his arm from its socket, but still the sword did not fall from Tarik's hand. Tarik reached with his free hand and, while trying to keep the beast's fangs from the hand that held the sword, grabbed the beast's one eye and twisted it with all the strength he could summon. For a long moment the two were frozen in combat at the water's edge as the beast strained against Tarik to force him into the water and Tarik twisted the eye that throbbed and twitched in his hand.

The slime from the socket rolled like hot lava down his arm, and then the eye, with a great popping sound, came loose in Tarik's hand. There was a horrible scream from the open mouth of the beast. Tarik, realizing that the sword was again loose, pulled it back and plunged it down into the creature's throat. The beast quivered and thrashed about, and then was still.

Tarik pushed the carcass away and climbed onto the shore. He wanted to rest, to sleep, but more than anything else he wanted to leave that awful place. He trotted around the edge of the lake until he reached the place where he had first knelt. He turned back for one last look and saw that the beast had stirred anew, and even then was probing the muddy ground for its lost eye.

Tarik took a deep breath and mounted his horse. Once he had gained the saddle, he started to put the Crystal into the bag that had held the fruit given him by Stria. The Crystal was heavier than he had thought it should be by the look of it. Sitting astride the horse, he cupped the Crystal in both hands before him and peered into it. At first he saw nothing, but then there was an image, and he raised the Crystal to look closer.

What he saw in the Crystal made him catch his breath sharply. For there was an image of his father, standing in the circle as El Muerte slowly approached. And there Tarik stood, away from the awful gaze of El Muerte, rooted in fear to the spot, a thought flickering through his mind like distant starlight on a rainy night, a thought half new, half remembered, that on that dread, sun-drenched day he had hoped they might not kill the boys when they had finished with the men.

Tarik, his eyes stinging with tears, lifted the Crystal to hurl it back into the water. But the weight of it made it fall short, and he saw it land among some bushes. He wanted to turn away from it and leave but knew he could not return to the Gardens of Shange without it. The beast still flopped about, groping for its eye. Soon it would find it, Tarik knew. He urged his horse forward and, leaning over in the saddle, scooped up the Crystal and started back toward the Gardens of Shange.

When he arrived back at the gardens, it was Docao who greeted him with fruit and cool water. But Tarik wanted neither and told Docao that he was weary and would go to his room. Docao looked into his eyes and saw the sadness there.

"Did you think it would be easy, little brother?" Docao began to pace as he spoke. "We are not meant to be giants, but just the frail creatures we are. And when we do rise above ourselves, we are shocked to find we long for the weaknesses we have shed. We are not heroic because of

69

our strengths, little brother, but in spite of them."

Tarik walked away from Docao, who did not seem to heed his going. He turned once to see the old man still pacing, still talking, still waving his good hand in the evening air to emphasize the words that fell about him.

Tarik went into the darkness of his room and, for the first time since he had begun his training, wept. He had somehow been able to forget the moment the Crystal had brought back, when his fear had turned his heart away from his father. None of Docao's words had brought comfort to him or eased the pain that he felt. He remembered saying to Docao that he had wished to avenge the death of his father, and now he wondered if it was the father's fall, or the son's, that pushed him on.

As Tarik sat huddled in the darkness, no answers came to him. He knew that he would sleep and rise again with no clearer vision of who he had been on the day of his father's death, and that any solace must come from who he was to be, come the morning.

SEVEN

"THERE ARE WONDERS IN THIS WORLD," NONGO SAID, "of which men have heard tales and which fill their thoughts with wonder. But for most men the tales are just that, tales that live like dreams remembered but never dreamed. The pursuit of such a dream will be your last task."

"I see," Tarik answered.

"I see . . ." Nongo repeated the words that Tarik had spoken, turning his head sideways as if to hear them better. "There is no excitement in your bosom, little brother, no eagerness."

"I think," Tarik said slowly, "that the pursuit of dreams is the work of children."

"Well, indeed." Nongo smiled. "But it is a sad testament that the experience of life results so surely in the death of innocence. Nevertheless, we will go on. Did I speak to you of wonders?"

"Wonders and dreams," Tarik said.

"Then let me fill your young head with an old black

dream," Nongo said. He picked up his beads and rolled them in the palm of his hand and then, as he spoke, between his thumb and fingertips.

"A long time ago, in the beginning of the beginning, before the footprint of man had ever been left by the banks of the Nile or had followed his shadow across the land of Punt, there was a being called Si, neither man nor god, but a force greater than the mind can grasp. It was Si who looked to the heavens and challenged the Great Spirit to a test of powers. When he had done this, he reached out and from a handful of sand created the passage of one moment unto the next. He held time high above his head and named it Time.

"When the Great Spirit saw this, he reached down and took into his hand the dust beneath Si's feet, and from this dust he created a living creature above all others, and he raised it above his head and called it Man.

"It was clear that the Great Spirit had won the test, for it was man who ruled Time. But to make the contest more equal, Si created Death, so that Time would once again rule man. When the Great Spirit saw this, He was so vexed that He changed Si into a horse with no memory of his former greatness, and named him Zinzinbadio."

"Zinzinbadio?" Tarik looked into Nongo's face.

"He is faster than any beast alive, running in great leaps that cover the length of three tall men, and he is strong enough to run from sunrise to sunset without tiring."

"And I am to capture this creature?" Tarik asked.

"Yes," Nongo answered. "To do so you must only mingle the sweat of your brow with the sweat that drips from the mane of this great horse. He is huge, but you will be tall enough to reach his mane."

"And how will I catch him to do this?" Tarik asked.

"Your wits will give you answers," Nongo said. "As you have learned not to turn from evil and to risk the truth, you must also learn to rely upon your mind.

"Your mind is keen, Tarik. You have only to free it from the channel of your past days and it will do what you ask of it."

Again Docao prepared a map for Tarik, telling him where he would find the prize of his last quest.

"Here"—Docao placed the stump of his arm on the center of the map—"you will find a large grassy plain. If the horse is not there when you arrive, you must wait for him. He will come with his herd, but there will be no mistaking him for just another beast. Go now and be well."

Tarik was given a horse by Docao and was told to treat it gently. It was not much of a horse, older than most and stiff-legged. The distance Tarik had to travel this time was great, giving him much time to think about what lay ahead for him. Nongo and Docao had told him to travel chiefly at night, so that he would not be discovered by any of El Muerte's warriors. This Tarik did, finding densely wooded areas in which to hide himself and sleep in the daytime.

There was something in the air that disturbed him. If he had been home, near the Niger that he had so loved as a child, he would have thought that it signaled the coming of the rainy season, for the air was heavy and chilled him to his very marrow. And sometimes he would wake and listen to the wind blowing softly, imagining that he heard something in its cold breath, something that was not clear no matter how hard he strained his ears to listen.

The shadows were growing shorter, and the summer sun beat down harshly on the plain. In the center was a stand of small trees and, just beyond, a hilly knoll. It had taken Tarik seventeen nights' travel to reach the place. The horse had grown more unwilling each day, and Tarik himself had felt more alone than he had since the time he first awakened at the Gardens of Shange to know that his father and brother were dead.

He tied his horse to a gnarled stump of a tree and sat and stared across the empty plain. It was here that he would see and capture Zinzinbadio.

Tarik waited the entire first day without seeing either another human being or a horse. A small gathering of birds twittered across the plain, now and then diving into the tall grass for insects and taking off again, catching the sun with their wings for a moment before turning black against the clear blue sky.

The night came and there were cicadas, chirping in a thousand rhythms until the coolness descended and the wind rose. Tarik pulled his robes closer to him and listened to the strange sound of the wind.

The next day came, and the rising sun was warm against Tarik's dark face. On the far edge of the plain, when the sun was at its highest, an old man passed, carrying a bundle of cane on his shoulder.

When the sun was halfway down and the day's warmth

had put Tarik nearly to sleep, he was suddenly awakened by the neighing of the horse. He looked up to see if the animal was still tied to the stump. Tarik thought at first that the horse might have been hungry, but he saw that there was plenty of grass still around the stump.

"Does the time grow heavy for you, too?" he asked the horse. He was pleased to hear the sound of his own voice. He decided to sing a song he had heard many times as a child; it was one that he had heard at his mother's knee.

The cup of your smile, coo, coo
Holds my morning meal, coo, coo
The fire in your eyes, coo, coo
Keeps the beast away, coo, coo
coo, coo, cu-roo, coo, coo, cu-roo
It must be that you are my child.

Tarik had just closed his eyes again when the horse neighed and stamped its hoof heavily on the ground. The song on Tarik's lips stopped in mid-note, and he opened his eyes in alarm. On the far side of the plain there was a cloud of dust that rose and moved across the line of Tarik's sight. He took a moment to look to both his left and right. There was nothing else to disturb the tranquillity of the horizon, so he turned his attention once again to the cloud.

As it neared, he saw that it was a small herd of horses. Ahead of them, moving almost without effort, there was a great black animal that Tarik knew was Zinzinbadio. The beauty and strength of the animal forced Tarik to catch his breath. Never had he seen such a magnificent beast. The horses behind him were galloping quickly, straining to keep up with their ebony leader. Tarik mounted his own horse. He sat on the animal without moving as his eyes stayed on Zinzinbadio.

The herd moved about the plain, first in one direction and then the next. Sometimes they would stop to graze or to cavort playfully among the trees that stood in the center of the plain. When one of the horses wandered too far from the body of the herd, Zinzinbadio nipped it on its flank and sent it back to the main body.

As Tarik watched this, a plan came to mind. He spurred his horse and headed slowly toward the herd. There would be no reason for speed, for the speed of his horse was not half that of Zinzinbadio. He allowed his horse to canter easily, stopping now and again, before resuming the slow approach. The herd did not react to him until he had nearly reached them. Then, seemingly without signal, they sprinted off to another part of the plain, with Zinzinbadio at their head.

Tarik saw that Zinzinbadio was some distance from the herd, but Tarik made no move toward him. Instead he again moved slowly toward the body of the herd, seeking that place farthest from the great horse. Again, when he had almost reached the herd, they sprinted away, this time stopping at a lesser distance than the first time. Tarik did not stop his horse, but merely turned it in the direction of the herd and let it proceed as slowly as before. When he again approached the herd, he saw that all the horses were magnificent animals, although none matched Zinzinbadio either in size or bearing. When the horses moved away from Tarik again, they moved away less quickly, as Tarik had hoped they would, and again Tarik slowly followed them, never moving in the direction of Zinzinbadio.

Out of the corner of his eye he could see Zinzinbadio, his head held high, the wind lifting his mane from the thick neck, the powerful legs prancing in place, ready to dart away.

This time Tarik reached the herd, and they did not move away. Surely Zinzinbadio knew that the herd could be quickly away from this slow-moving horse and rider. Some of the other horses neighed nervously when Tarik stopped some short distance from the herd. Tarik sat as still as he could in the saddle. Zinzinbadio moved away again, and Tarik, after waiting until the rest of the herd began to move, followed.

This he did for the rest of the day and even when the sun had set. When the horses went among the trees that evening, Tarik saw that Zinzinbadio did not go with them. Tarik went with the herd and spent the night with them. On the second day on the plain Tarik did the same thing that he had done on the first, moving always with the herd, never close to Zinzinbadio. But on the evening of the second day he moved away from the herd and away from Zinzinbadio. For a long time the great black horse ignored Tarik, but finally he approached Tarik's horse and snorted. When he did this, Tarik spurred his animal ever so gently back toward the herd.

Tarik had reasoned that it would take several more days to get Zinzinbadio used to having him with his herd. But by the third day Tarik found himself growing weak with hunger. The sun beating down on him made his head ache and played tricks with his eyesight. He knew that his time to sit on the horse without resting or eating had grown short.

He sat now in the middle of the herd. His lips were parched and dry, and he wondered how much strength he had left. Slowly he raised his hand to his forehead and felt the perspiration forming as the day grew warmer. He looked down at the shadows, not daring to peer into the brilliant sky, and realized that the sun was nearing its peak. It was the time either to accomplish his mission or to fail. His legs were almost numb from sitting on the horse, and it was with more effort than he had thought would be necessary that he turned and pressed his horse with his knees and feet away from the herd, pushing the horse into a gallop.

At first he thought that his plan would not work. But soon there was, in the corner of his eye, a blur that grew quickly. It was Zinzinbadio coming toward him to bring the horse back to the herd. Tarik turned his horse again, away from the oncharging black steed bearing down upon him. Zinzinbadio was quickly closing the distance between them, and now Tarik urged his own animal on.

He looked under his arm as he rode and saw that Zinzinbadio was gaining, and almost as soon as he had seen this, the horse was alongside of him. Tarik's horse grew frightened and tried to turn back toward the herd, but Tarik spurred the horse and held the reins tightly until his arms were aching and his hands raw. Then Zinzinbadio came closer. With one motion Tarik wiped the sweat from his face and reached out and grabbed Zinzinbadio by the mane. The mighty horse shook his head once, twice—and Tarik found himself flying through the air, falling hard on the ground. But he had done what he had been bade to do—mingled his sweat with that of Zinzinbadio.

The pain in his shoulder where he had landed throbbed relentlessly, and the sun filled him with a confusion of light and pain. When he came to his senses, he looked around him and saw that his horse had run off in the direction of the herd. But there, a short distance away, pawing at the ground, stood the great Zinzinbadio. Tarik stood up slowly, his heart pounding with excitement and exhaustion, and walked toward the great animal.

Zinzinbadio reared and pawed the air. He snorted and jumped, arching his back as he did so. But when Tarik had reached him, he stopped and neighed. Tarik took a deep breath, put his two hands on the animal's back, and lifted himself up. All the way back to the Gardens of Shange he spoke soothingly to the horse, and when he put his hands on the animal's head and saw how the color of the horse exactly matched his own, he knew that it was good.

When Tarik arrived back at the Gardens of Shange, it was Docao who greeted him with a glad cry.

"It is Tarik!" Docao cried. "He has returned!"

"Does he walk or does he ride?" Nongo asked.

"He rides in triumph!" Docao announced. "In utter and glorious triumph!"

Docao had cleaned out the small stable and had raised its door so that Zinzinbadio would fit therein. Tarik was pleased when he saw this and still more pleased when, later, it was Docao who brought him baked lamb and currants for his dinner. Tarik ate the meal offered to him and drank a goblet of cold spring water and was pleased with himself.

"Where is Nongo?" Tarik asked when the meal was finished.

"He is in his room," Docao replied. "He is tired. It is not easy waiting upon your successes."

"They are easy," Tarik said, rising from the large table.

He bade Docao good night and started to his own room to rest, for the relaxation of the meal had allowed his weariness to descend upon him heavily. Still, he was full of the day and of his adventure in capturing Zinzinbadio. He went to where he knew Nongo's room to be and tapped lightly on the door.

"Enter."

Tarik had never before been in Nongo's room and was shocked at its sparseness. There was a single mat that lay against one wall, and a cup filled with water near the head of it. The gray twilight, filtering through the slatted window, cast shadows on the stone floor that moved with the late evening breeze, and Tarik imagined the shadows to be of the gauntly twisted sycamore that stood a mute guard outside.

"I came to bid you good night," Tarik said.

"Good night?" Nongo lay stretched on the mat, bare to the waist, his thin arms supporting his body in a semi-upright position. "For a blind man only death is night, little brother. But I thank you for your thoughts."

"You know that it went very well for me?" Tarik asked.

"So Docao has told me."

"I feel that I could fulfill a hundred quests," Tarik said.

"As many as that?" Nongo smiled. "Perhaps. But now it is time for you to do what you have been training to do for so many seasons. Now we shall see if the gods smile upon you."

"It will be like the others," Tarik said, sitting on the floor by Nongo's side. "Tomorrow I will practice with the sword again. I am already nearly perfect."

"No, there will be no more practice," Nongo said. "Tomorrow you must leave."

"Tomorrow? Why so soon?"

"For many reasons," Nongo answered. "We grow too fond of you and you of us. Nor can I delude you that what you have done will be sufficient to defeat El Muerte. It will not be easy."

"How can he stand against me?" Tarik asked. "Does he have a horse as marvelous as Zinzinbadio? A sword like Serq? Such a Crystal as I have? Without these things he will fall."

"With them you will fall unless you bring to them such a spirit as will overcome his great evil. The fly that is trapped in the spider's web sees the logic of the web and thinks it is the same world that he has left behind. But it is the spider that is real and not the web.

"Now you must get some sleep so that you will be fresh for your journey," Nongo said.

"Tell me first of your home," Tarik said, not wanting to leave. "I have told you of mine."

"No, no." Nongo shook his head. "If I were to wander down those paths again, we would not sleep until this time tomorrow."

"Tell me how you came to know Docao," Tarik said, shifting his position.

"How I came to meet him?" Nongo tilted his chin and thought for a moment. "We met in the valley of our lives. There is little more to say. But you must be tired."

"It won't matter if I sit and talk with you more," Tarik said. "I can rest tomorrow."

"Does leaving bother you?" Nongo asked.

"Not if you think I am ready," Tarik said.

"Not if I think . . . ?" Nongo drew his legs up slowly and lifted himself to his knees. "Little brother, take my hand."

Tarik took Nongo's right hand in his own right hand and held it firmly.

"I have it, Nongo," he said.

"The hand is moist."

"The room is warm," Tarik said.

"The hand weeps with the wonder of tomorrow, but it is strong," Nongo said. "It is strong."

"Then you think I am ready?" Tarik asked.

"Only you can know when you are ready, Tarik," Nongo answered, "not I. If I could tear the griefs I have known in this land from my soul and put them into your face as the scars of passage from childhood to manhood, I would, but I cannot. There is no shadow of pain that I can give you, no charm saved for this moment, no forbidden lodge to take you to. We are far from that land, and from that day of blood and ritual that would have whispered your destiny to you. No, you must close your eyes as a child this night and open them into manhood without mystery or fire. Wash your hands well before you sleep, and dream in peace, little brother."

Tarik released Nongo's hand and put his arms around the old man. Nongo embraced him warmly, the tears stinging his blind eyes in the gathering darkness.

"Go, little brother, the hour is late."

Tarik, filled again with the weariness of his efforts that day and setting his mind for what the new day was to bring, rose quickly and went to his room.

EIGHT

WHEN HE AWOKE THE NEXT MORNING TARIK SAW that Docao and Nongo had not prepared breakfast for him. He bathed and went into the gardens, and there he found them huddled over a small table.

"Good morning, little brother," Docao said. "Come see what we have prepared for you."

When he approached the table, Tarik saw a tunic fashioned of leather and covered from shoulder to knee with mail. There was a helmet, too, also of leather and covered with mail. The inside of the helmet was fashioned of sheep's wool.

"It is not so heavy as to encumber you, little brother," Docao said, "but it will give you some protection against lesser enemies."

"It is good," said Tarik. He ran his fingers along the well-oiled leather and then over the rough mail. It was indeed good.

"You must try it on," Nongo said, "so that we can know if it fits you well. Tonight you must be on your

84

journey. We have given you as much as we can. From this moment we have nothing more to give."

Tarik tried on the garment and found that it fit quite well. He ate his morning meal and spent the rest of the day sitting quietly. In the afternoon he saw to Zinzinbadio, feeding the horse and brushing his coat. Then he went to his room and slept until it was time to leave.

When he awoke, the moon was shining through silver-gray clouds. In the distance he could hear the crash of thunder reverberating through the hills.

"It is nearly time, little brother." Docao spoke the words through the arched doorway.

Tarik did not answer. He dressed quickly, doused his face with cold water from the urn on his table, and went into the gardens, where Docoa, Nongo, and Stria waited.

They had made adjustments to the tunic. He put it on and it fitted him perfectly. Still they probed here and there, adjusting this strap and then the next, and Tarik sensed that they did not want the evening to grow, but wanted somehow to stop the moon in its flight across the sky. There was a light sprinkle of rain.

Docao put his arm around Tarik's neck and drew him close. He began to whisper into Tarik's ear. The words came in a torrent, and although they were in a tongue foreign to Tarik, he knew they were words of Docao's relationship to his god. Tarik bowed his head in respect and did not move until Docao had finished. Then Docao kissed Tarik on both sides of his face and looked deeply into his eyes.

"Little brother, there is much weight upon your shoul-

85

ders," he said. "Know that no matter how great the evil there is also a good, and a God who protects that good." Then he made the sign of the cross before Tarik. "May the Lord and His good be with you always." And he kissed Tarik once more, upon the forehead. "I will go to get Zinzinbadio."

Then Tarik turned to Nongo, who now sat still upon the ground, looking smaller than ever. The rain began to fall harder. Tarik knelt on the wet ground next to Nongo.

"You will be in my heart as I go on my journey," he said. "I will keep with me those things that you have said. Be well until I return."

Nongo lifted his face to Tarik. A bolt of lightning streaked across the sky, lighting up the black face and the lifeless eyes from which tears now rolled freely.

"Son of Alkebu-lan"—Nongo spoke slowly—"I have called upon the spirits of my ancestors to help you in your tasks, and Docao has called upon his God. And beyond this we have called upon the powers of light and darkness, even with the risk of hell bearing down upon us. Do not fail us, or the spirits of your own ancestors who cry for vengeance. Do not let this evil triumph."

"I will not fail," Tarik said. "Look how the sky calls out on the night I start my search for El Muerte. It is a good omen."

"No." Nongo bowed his head. "Docao tells me that in the sky to the east a streak of fire sped across the sky. That is an omen that one person who fights against evil will die. It is not a good omen, my son."

Zinzinbadio pranced nervously as Docao led him into

the gardens. Tarik saw that they had made a covering for him like the one that Tarik himself wore. Tarik clasped Nongo to him, and then, in turn, Docao. He looked also for the girl, but she had gone.

The Crystal was in his pouch tied around his waist, and Serq was by his side. Tarik breathed deeply and then mounted Zinzinbadio.

"Travel northward, little brother," Docao called to him through the rain that now began to beat more heavily upon the earth. "You will hear word of him whom you seek, it is assured."

Tarik lifted his hand to wave good-bye. As he did so, there was a sudden orange light in the eastern sky. It was a second fireball.

A slight movement of his heels against Zinzinbadio's flanks and Tarik was on his way. As he passed through the archway that led from the Gardens of Shange, he did not look back.

The path along which he traveled was narrow and winding, but Zinzinbadio had little trouble following it. The rain was cold and chilled Tarik to the bone. He tried not to think of the fireballs that flew across the sky. Was it so sure that he would die? Just as he raised his hand, one had streaked across the night sky. He remembered another hand being raised—that of his father as he lifted his arm against the falling blow of El Muerte's sword. He felt an anger well in his bowels that he had not felt for a long time. And when this came, this anger, he made up his mind that if he did die, it would not be in vain.

"Where my blood touches the earth," he said to Zinzinbadio, "there also shall spill the blood of El Muerte."

He rode on through the rain, allowing his mind to drift back to a time when he was a small boy and his father had held him in the water as they bathed in the river not far from their home. His father would hold him and then plunge them both under the water. When he stood upright again his father would be laughing. Tarik remembered the water coming off his father's sparkling teeth as he threw his head back in laughter. He remembered, too, how he had imagined that, because the sun seemed always to shine when his father played with him or worked in the marketplace, and would go down when his father slept, somehow his father had controlled the sun.

It was in the middle of such a thought that the crackle of lightning, hissing above his head and followed almost instantaneously by a huge clap of thunder, revealed what looked like a horseman up the road. Tarik thought that it might have been his imagination as he peered into the darkness. There was something there, but it could have been a tree or a bush. He felt himself tense as he neared it. The rain had slowed again to a light drizzle, but the chill remained.

The bobbing of the head revealed that it was a horse, and Tarik drew his sword. He stopped Zinzinbadio and waited for the horseman to make himself known. It was then that the moon came from behind the clouds and cast a dim light on the rider. It was Stria! He looked at her and saw that she stared back at him with the same fierce eyes he had seen in the Gardens of Shange. He moved

Zinzinbadio closer to her, replacing his sword in its scabbard.

She was wrapped completely in a shawl and looked almost like a mound of rags balanced on the saddle of her horse.

"What are you doing here?" Tarik asked.

She did not respond for a long moment, but merely returned his gaze as steadily as he gave it. Then she opened the shawl, and Tarik saw that she was bare-legged, in the manner of a young boy. Nor did she wear anything on her arms. But over her body was the same tunic of mail and leather that had been fashioned for him. Around her neck hung a dagger in a thin sheath. She wore it in much the same fashion that Docao wore a cross around his neck. When Tarik had seen these things, Stria closed her shawl.

"You must return to the gardens," Tarik said.

Stria did not move. A flash of lightning illuminated her face. Her dark hair stuck to the sides of her face, and the rain glistened in the corners of her slightly parted lips.

"Return to the gardens!" Tarik lifted his voice above the rain and wind, but still Stria did not move.

Tarik pressed his knees into Zinzinbadio's flanks and turned the horse northward again. He did not have to look back to know that the girl would be behind him.

PART TWO

nine

AL CAZABA DEL TIBERIUS WAS A SMALL WAY STATION once used by the Romans on the long road that traveled southward to Traducta. It was this place that El Muerte had taken and fashioned into a castle that he felt suited his rank as head of a royal army. It was situated in a spot made arid by the gradual diversion of a freshwater tributary that had once run along its north side and that now turned abruptly away from the place a half mile to the west. But its barrenness was no hindrance to El Muerte. He rather enjoyed the sparseness of the land and saw it as an easy place to defend if the need arose. Also, the meanness of Al Cazaba offered the royal family of Naed, in whose employ El Muerte found himself, some assurance that their power was not being challenged by the fierce leader of their army. Still, there was an uneasiness between the royal family and El Muerte. When an envoy from the royal family arrived at the castle of El Muerte, there arose such a tension in the air that even the lowliest foot soldier could feel it. The tension bothered El Muerte, who knew that one day it would come to a meeting of wills between himself and the prince he served. He knew, however, that if the time of conflict could be of his own choosing, he could rule the day.

Now he sat brooding in the large marble tub, eating the black olives that Jad the Unclean, the small white creature, said to be but part human, took from the shallow silver chalice and placed, one by one, in his mouth. The glowing ash from the pine logs was all that was left of the fire that had been raging when the Prince's envoy had arrived that day. When the envoy had finished with his lengthy discourse and had retired for the night, El Muerte had summoned his brother, Jefrod, and Daaro, the captain of his guard, to his side. They had entered his room, and he had gestured for them to sit, which they had. He had not spoken since that moment, and neither the captain nor El Muerte's younger brother dared to break the silence, lest they incur his wrath. Finally, long past the moment when the silence seemed unbearable, El Muerte pushed Jad's hand away from him and spoke.

"There was no omen to warn me of such unhappy tidings," he said, half mumbling the words into his chest. "First there is news of some black knight who wishes me harm . . . what grudge does he bear me?"

"I do not know"—the captain of the guard licked his lips between words—"but it is said that he is of the blacks we brought from the south, sire."

"And . . . ?"

"Some were killed and others sold."

"I hear he is some sort of demon." El Muerte lifted his

94

hands from the water and watched the clear liquid run down his huge arms. "Is this true?"

"I would imagine so, sire. They say he has a special sword—"

"With which he is going to stand against me?" El Muerte's smile was like a white wound in the belly of a whale. "I will enjoy killing him. He will be a moment's diversion when I have time. Enough of him now. Speak to me again those words that the Prince's envoy spoke."

"Unhappy." Jad the Unclean jumped to his feet and slapped his knees to get the blood circulating again. "The Prince has heard reports that the people are unhappy. They say that they have been treated badly. More taxes are taken away than is fair to them."

"Jefrod, come sit by my side and hold my hand and tell me what I shall do." El Muerte extended a hand toward his younger brother. Jad the Unclean quickly dried it off before Jefrod reached it and took it in his own.

"It is not the Prince who causes these evils to come about, brother," Jefrod said. "It is his aunt. Since the King's death she whispers in the boy's ear both night and day."

"Have we inherited such sins from our father that she should hate us so?" El Muerte asked. "How have we harmed this woman?"

"She wishes to marry him to one of the royal families in the north—"

"The Franks, no doubt." El Muerte spat into the water.

"But it is well known that the Prince's only trump is the strength of his army. Your strength is boon and bane to her, as is her ambition to you," Jefrod said. "Power breeds its own enemies."

"Is it possible that you could travel to the Prince with the envoy and deliver to him the message of my solicitude to both him and his people?"

"If it is your wish," Jefrod replied.

"To be truthful, it is not really my most earnest wish," El Muerte said. "I fear they will not treat you with respect."

"I will go with your blessing," Jefrod said.

"But be aware that it may not all be flaws in their thinking, brother. I once professed a love for the Prince that I can no longer feel. If I have revealed my changed feelings, perhaps he or the woman sees it as enmity. In truth, I have been so busy with my duties and so full of their importance that I hold love in my heart only for you and the memory of our parents. All others are distant. It is a fault that causes me grief, but one that can be repaired as time proves my intention."

"Shall I go ahead of the envoy?" Jefrod asked. "I will take gifts of silver and plead before the envoy returns with his tales."

"No," El Muerte said. "Your actions might be considered subterfuge. Travel with the envoy in the morning. Kiss me and sleep well tonight."

Jefrod kissed his brother and left. El Muerte signaled Jad to his side, and the small man came, blinking furiously, and washed his master's face.

"Jefrod is right," El Muerte said. "It is not the Prince but the old hag. She watches from behind his shoulder like the ugly, wrinkled vulture she is. How I would love to strangle her before a mirror so she could watch herself die."

"The envoy does her bidding as well." The captain of the guard ventured to speak. "Whatever my master does they will twist between them until it is poisoned."

"No, I will send a message that cannot be poisoned." El Muerte lifted Jad and brought him into the tub. "When Jefrod and the envoy set out on their journey to deliver my salutations, they will be set upon and killed by the very peasants who cry against me. Their deaths will prove that it is the peasants who are evil, and not me. You will see to the arrangements."

"Yes, sire." The captain stood up. "Your brother is to be . . . ?"

"He was always useless." El Muerte had taken Jad the Unclean on his lap and was combing his hair. "Did I tell you that my father believed his birth to be the cause of my mother's melancholy?"

"No, sire."

"It is true," El Muerte said. "It is true."

"Yes, sire."

"And give the silver that he carries to the peasants—no, give a third of it to the peasants. Perhaps we have been harsh with them."

TEN

MUCH TIME HAD PASSED BETWEEN THAT MOMENT when Tarik witnessed the death of his father and the time he pushed northward to begin his search for El Muerte. It was a time in which he had become something else than what he had been. His body had grown hard and his hand quick. It had been a passage from youth to manhood that should have been made in the footsteps of his father and of his uncles and of his peoples along the comforting Niger.

He had been captured as a boy and brought to this land, and now, after less than two turnings of the seasons, it was as a man that he sought the one who had brought him to the grief he had borne for so long. He had been told by Docao and Nongo that the wind would bring him news of El Muerte's whereabouts, and Tarik thought again of the time when the wind had brought news of El Muerte's coming to Oulata, and so he rode and listened.

He traveled northward until he reached Epora, and then, skirting the edge of that town, he continued in a direction more to the east and away from the unsettled plains. He was wary, even in his great confidence, and let nothing pass him unnoticed.

"Do not close your eyes when you do not sleep," Docao had warned him, "for a danger unseen is a knife at the heart."

Tarik did not travel quickly. He stopped now and again to talk to people of the land who journeyed alone or in pairs, or to the shepherds who tended their flocks along the hilly countryside. He could see that at first they feared him and often did not believe that he was not one of El Muerte's men. They were careful not to speak of El Muerte or, if they did, to do so with careful praise for fear that Tarik was his agent. But what little was said was enough for Tarik to learn in which direction he must go to seek his enemy.

Stria followed at a distance, and Tarik did nothing further to discourage her. In truth it pleased him to see her coming over the rise of a hill or appearing almost ghostlike from the early morning mists. There were times when he would have liked to have had her ride beside him, but he knew that was not her way.

On the fifth day from the Gardens of Shange he happened upon a shepherd boy who tended a few sheep and some goats outside a small village. The village itself looked inviting—a gathering of white homes with red tiled roofs that snuggled along a shallow tributary. The houses were garlanded with flowers of all colors and seemed to breathe with light and cleanliness.

Tarik saw the shepherd boy and rode toward him. The

boy did not move as Tarik brought Zinzinbadio to a halt a few feet from him. Tarik looked down at the boy and saw that he was not much older than his brother Umeme had been. The boy looked up from where he was sitting and nervously fingered the bamboo flute he held.

"How are you called?" Tarik asked, dismounting slowly.

"Acinto," the boy said.

"Your sheep are fine animals," Tarik told him.

"Will you take them away?" The boy's wide eyes were turned on Tarik.

"They are not mine," Tarik said. "Why should I take them?"

"The tax collectors take what they want," the boy replied. "They have sent word that they come today. Are you not with them?"

"Does it appear that I am?" Tarik asked.

"You are dressed much as they are dressed," the boy replied. "Only you are black of face."

"I am not one of them," Tarik said. "To whom do you pay tithes?"

"The Prince," the boy replied. "They say he lives to the north, near a place called Olcades. That is where his castle is. But it is not he who comes to take the taxes, it is the soldiers of Artia who come. They are very cruel. They take too much, but no one dares stand against them."

"Artia?" Tarik asked. "He is a soldier?"

"He does not wear the uniform of a soldier," the boy replied. "But they say he is very fierce."

"They only *say?*" Tarik smiled. "You have never seen him?"

"Few people have seen El Muerte," the boy half mumbled. "They say it is best to hide when he comes."

Tarik felt his stomach tense at the mention of El Muerte. He did not speak again to the boy, but turned his eyes toward the town. The boy moved a few inches away from Tarik. When Tarik looked toward him, he tried to smile but could not. Tarik saw the fear in the boy's face.

"What is the name of this town?" Tarik asked.

"Mentifsa," the boy replied.

Tarik ran the palm of his hand along the wide neck of Zinzinbadio. Then he mounted slowly and started toward the town.

Though the surrounding countryside rolled lavishly in waves of green fields along the banks of the two rivers that converged to the north, Mentifsa itself was mostly flat and depended on its one stream for fish and to turn a small grist mill. Tarik could feel the stares of the people as he allowed Zinzinbadio to pick his own way through the narrow, winding streets. Several shops were open, and untended chickens and game hens roamed freely in and out of the doorways.

The center of the town consisted of stone wells situated in the midst of a shrub garden. On either side of the square that contained the wells was a church. The churches were the same except that in one of them the tower seemed incomplete. There were few people in the streets, and those who were there went about their tasks quickly and did not look in Tarik's direction. But Tarik knew that he was, nevertheless, being watched. He could feel the eyes behind the shuttered windows and between the cracks over the heavy brass-studded doors of the low dwellings.

Tarik stopped at the well and drew water for himself, and then some for Zinzinbadio. He stood near the horse when he had finished drinking and looked around for someone to speak to, but as soon as his eyes met those of another, the person would turn quickly away. No one neared the well as he stood there. Occasionally a door would open and someone would come out with a bucket but would stop at sight of Tarik. He mounted Zinzinbadio and moved away from the well to the shade of an ancient sprawling sycamore, where he would not be so obvious. Two old women ventured to the well to draw water, looking nervously in Tarik's direction as they did so.

Tarik considered leaving and returning to the field in which he had seen the shepherd boy and speaking once again to him. The boy seemed as frightened as the townspeople, but Tarik thought that, because he was younger, he might overcome his fear more easily and speak with him freely. As he was weighing these thoughts, he heard the sound of approaching horses and saw the few townspeople who were out go quickly into their houses and close the heavy brass-studded doors behind them. Three soldiers on horseback entered the square from the far side, away from Tarik. Behind them another soldier rode in an ox cart. Tarik stepped back into the shadows of the tree.

When the ox cart had stopped in front of the first house that bordered the square, the doors immediately opened and a man and a woman emerged, carrying between them a large basket, which they loaded onto the cart. One of the soldiers looked into the basket and then sent the couple away with a wave of his hand. From the next house came a man and a child carrying kegs of wine and a small chest. The wine was put on the cart, and the soldiers eagerly opened the chest and split its contents among themselves. It was clear to Tarik that these were the tax collectors of whom the boy had spoken.

A short roundish man and an even fatter but taller woman were next. They brought some cloth and put that on the cart as well as several loaves of round bread. The soldiers spoke to them and held up several fingers.

"No, it is enough!" the man cried out. The woman jumped back, alarmed. She immediately started to run, as best she could, toward the house.

One of the soldiers had a heavy staff, and he swung it and hit the man across the back. There was a great cloud that came from the man's blouse as he fell to the ground. The soldier hit him again. The woman returned, carrying more cloth for the tax collectors.

"No, it is enough!" The man had regained his feet and ran up to the woman, spreading his arms before her so that she would give no more to the tax collector.

A heavy blow on the back knocked the man down again. The woman dropped the cloth and, holding her head with her hands, dropped to her knees at his side. One of the soldiers grabbed her quickly and pulled her away. The others began to beat the man, and Tarik saw that one of them had drawn his sword.

Almost before he realized it himself, Tarik had leaped onto Zinzinbadio and had moved into the square.

"Hold!" he commanded

The soldier who had drawn his sword stopped in midair and turned to face him. When he saw Tarik on Zinzinbadio, a sneer curled his mouth into an almost half smile.

"Look at this black thing that commands us to hold," he said to his comrades. "Shall we draw lots to see who cuts his tongue from his head?"

The other two soldiers stopped beating the man on the ground and turned toward Tarik.

"We don't draw lots," one of them said. "It is my due as befits my rank."

Tarik slipped to the ground and drew his own sword. The soldier charged directly at him, swinging his larger weapon wildly as he did so. Tarik parried the blow easily and brought his sword across the neck and shoulders of the soldier. The soldier gasped, dropped his weapon, and fell to the ground, dead. The second soldier came with a great ax. He had massive arms and brought the ax crashing toward Tarik's skull. Tarik sidestepped the blow and brought his sword up quickly. The cutting edge caught the soldier's wrist and separated the hand neatly from the arm. On the ground the hand, still clutching the ax, twitched in the afternoon dust.

In a blind fury, the now one-handed man drew his dagger with his left hand, but not in time to prevent Tarik from thrusting Serq deep into his belly.

The other two soldiers abandoned the cart and ran desperately away from the square toward where they had left their horses tied. The townspeople threw tomatoes at them and jeered as they ran.

"What can I say to you?" the man who had been beaten said to Tarik. "You have saved my life. All I own in this world belongs to you."

"Take your life, friend," Tarik said, "and your possessions. I haven't need of either. Perhaps you can tell me of a good place to spend the night and obtain a good meal."

"My house is yours," the man said. "Please, come with me."

As Tarik followed the man into the house, other people came from their homes to get a glimpse of him. Some touched him, others patted Zinzinbadio as they passed.

"My name is Capa," the man said when they had settled down at his table.

"Capa the fool!" the woman hissed as she brought steamy bowls of leek soup to the two men.

"This lovely creature is my wife, Maria," Capa said, shrugging.

"The wife of a fool!" Maria said, putting a piece of lamb in Tarik's soup.

"Am I a fool because I do not want to give everything I have in the world to the tax collector?" Capa asked. "Is this the thought of a foolish man? I work every day to make bread to sell. If the demands were reasonable, it would not be so bad. But each time the tax collectors come, they always want more and more. But enough about me. Where did such a brave knight as yourself come from?"

"From south of here," Tarik answered. "It doesn't really matter."

"Everyone will know about you soon enough," Maria said, putting the goods they had brought out to the wagon back onto the shelves. "After what you did today, every tongue will be clucking your name about."

"He is a brave man," Capa said. "Like me, I am a brave man, too. More brave than the others, who only rushed to bring more for them to take away."

"If he hadn't come along you would still be lying in the gutter," Maria said, wiping her hands on a cloth. "And maybe with a stout piece of steel through the middle of you."

"I would have had the best of them in a moment more," Capa said. "These hands are as strong as the paws of a bear. Remember that, woman!"

"Tell me about this Prince," Tarik asked.

"The Prince!" Capa snorted loudly and wiped his nose with the sleeve of his blouse. "He allows himself to be seen once or twice a year, and then only a peek from behind the curtains of the carriage that carries him. He is thin and as white as a ghost—how did you get so black?"

"Where I come from all the people are my color," Tarik answered.

"The rest of the year," Capa went on, "he sends his tax collectors to do his dirty work. They come and they take what they want. I'm sure more than a little of it goes into their own coffers. If you pay, they want more. If you do not pay, they beat you. Last spring a man—he was a good man—refused to pay. They beat him until he died. Since then no one has dared to stand up to them. Except me, of course. But I am a special man, even though I am not a knight like yourself."

"And El Muerte," Tarik asked, "tell me about him."

"Put the Devil on a horse with a feather behind his ear and what you have is that one!" Maria said. "Have some more bread."

"What the woman says is true," Capa said: "El Muerte is a bad one. He comes now and then, not too many times. But when he comes, he always leaves someone dead. This one looked at him with an evil eye, or that one fingered the handle of his knife as he passed. There is always some small reason, and someone who dies. After a while when he comes you do not think about how much he takes, you only hope that he does not decide to kill you."

"It is El Muerte I search for," Tarik said. "He killed my father with his own sword, and it was his men who killed my brothers, my sisters, and my mother."

Capa looked at his wife, who turned her head. There was a large pot over the fire, and the thick liquid in it bubbled softly. The sunlight through the door formed a large patch of gold on the dirt floor across which a small bug scurried. Maria wrung one large hand in the other.

"What do they call you, my brave black knight?" Capa asked.

"I am called Tarik."

"Tarik, it is a strong name," Capa said. "And you are a good man and fought very well against his soldiers. But defeating his soldiers is not the same as defeating El Muerte. My wife spoke of a devil on a horse. It is not just a way of saying things. We believe this to be true. This is an evil man, who delights in killing. To face him will be to throw away your life."

"We will see," Tarik answered.

There was a commotion outside, and Maria went to see what was going on. Capa put his arm on that of Tarik and bade him be still. A moment later Maria returned.

"What is the news, woman?" Capa asked.

"They are saying that the two soldiers who ran away today will be back tomorrow with others to capture the black one," Maria said. "The people in the town will say that he has gone south, the direction from which he came."

"It would not be a bad idea," Capa said. "Your horse looks like a magnificent animal. If you went south now, they would never catch up with you. You could hide among your own people."

"That is not my mission," Tarik answered. "If I may stay here tonight, I will begin my journey north again when dawn breaks."

"If it must be," Capa said, "it must be. Until then my home is your home. And you might as well know, in case they don't have bakers where you come from, there is no man more loved than a baker. The people in this town love me almost too much."

"Poof!" Maria blew in the direction of her husband.

"My family has been in this small town for as far back as we can remember, and we have always been bakers. We feed the people—that is why they love us. They would defend me with their lives. Do not let what you saw today mislead you, my friend. They only bide their time until the time is ready for them to rise.

"Hey, that's pretty good! They bide their time until it is time to *rise*. Like bread. Don't worry, it is not easy to catch on to. Bakers are very wise, so we can say these things easily."

Tarik and Capa talked long into the evening. Capa told of the things that he knew of El Muerte and how afraid the people were of him. Maria stayed with them until her eyes grew heavy with sleep and Capa had to awaken her to tell her to go to bed.

Capa drew a curtain over one side of his small house and made a pallet for Tarik to lie on. Tarik's own eyes were weary, too, and the idea of sleep was welcome to him. He first checked to see that Zinzinbadio was fed and comfortable, and then he removed his armor. He laid the armor neatly by the foot of his pallet and put his sword between himself and the wall. Next he took the Crystal of Truth and put it by his head.

"Good night, my friend," Capa called to him, "and pleasant dreams."

"Good night," Tarik replied.

Tarik put his head down and felt his body begin to relax. He became aware of a dull ache in his right knee and turned his body so there would be no weight on the leg. He remembered what Capa had said, about how bakers were loved. There was something bothersome about it, something that did not come immediately to mind, but it had been a full, tiring day, and Tarik quickly pushed it from his mind.

ELEVEN

SLEEP CAME FITFULLY, AND WITH IT A DREAM. HE dreamed that he had somehow reached the distant horizon and, sitting astride Zinzinbadio, he saw on one side of him the bright coming of the new day, and on the other the darkness of the night that had been. He sat as quietly as he could on Zinzinbadio and attempted to reach out with his being both to the darkness and the light, so that he might know the life about him. When he reached out, he felt the ebb and flow of life in all its forms—the trees, beasts stirring in their slumber, the rapid heartbeat of birds in their nests. But there was one area in which he could not feel, and it was here that he brought his attention. It was a boulder, the height of a tall man, that lay on the edge of a stand of trees. Tarik concentrated on the boulder, and gradually he felt a form huddled at its base. It was the lifeleless body of the soldier he had killed that afternoon. And as the form became known to him, Tarik seemed to diminish in both size and force, nor could he turn his mind away from the lifeless body. He tried to spur Zinzinbadio away, but the great horse seemed rooted to the spot.

Tarik awoke with a great start, the sweat dripping from his hands, his heart pounding. Remembering his dream, he trembled in the darkness.

He could not sleep again and turned uneasily on the uncomfortable pallet. He tried to interpret his dream but could not, finding no meaning that was clear. The small candle that Capa had left burning was almost exhausted, giving off, in its dying throes, an oily aroma that annoyed Tarik. He arose to extinguish the candle that flickered dimly near the pouch in which he kept the Crystal of Truth. The idea came to him that he might look into the Crystal for a meaning of his dream.

He took the Crystal from its pouch, let it rest briefly in the palm of his hand, and then held it up before the candle. What he saw made him sit upright.

"Capa! Capa!" he called out even as he sprang to his feet. He heard scurrying in the next room.

"What is it?" Capa called.

"Come and see," Tarik answered.

By the time Capa came, Tarik was fastening his armor.

"But I thought you weren't leaving until dawn," Capa said. "Why this sudden change of plans?"

Tarik handed the Crystal to Capa.

"Look into this Crystal," Tarik said. "What you see there will be truth."

Capa looked at the Crystal, squinted at it, and then held it up to the light. As he looked, his face changed expressions many times.

111

"I see people coming to take us," Capa said. "It is like dream pictures. I do not understand them. I know the people—it is Hans and Guerra from the marketplace—but what does it mean? Where are they taking us?"

"To El Muerte's men," Tarik said, tying on his sword. "They think they will be spared if they deliver us. Come, we must leave this place at once."

"But why will they take me?" Capa asked. "I did nothing to anyone. I am innocent!"

Tarik stopped and looked at the little round man for a long moment.

"Then stay here and tell them that you were the one I saved by killing their soldiers," Tarik said. "Tell them that you are innocent and wait for their answer."

"Enough," Capa said. "I know what that answer will be. I must kiss my wife good-bye."

Capa went in to his wife and spoke to her quickly. As he spoke he dressed, and she began to pray as quickly as she could, the words rushing from her lips and her hands fluttering across her ample breast.

"I hear them coming," Tarik said. "We must go now."

Capa, too, could hear the sound of the crowd as they approached his house. He and Tarik slipped quietly out of the house and made their way to where Zinzinbadio and Capa's horses were tied. In moments they were on their way. They rode far into the night, not stopping to rest or to speak to one another until the first rays of the sun glowed along the distant hilltops. Then they lay down and rested.

"Why would they do something like that?" Capa

112

moaned. "I thought they all hated El Muerte's men as much as I."

"El Muerte knew something that we did not," Tarik said. "That fear beats more loudly in a man's breast than courage."

"It is a wondrous thing, that Crystal you have," Capa said. "How did you come by it?"

"It was as difficult a task as one would imagine," Tarik replied. "If I had the same chance again, I doubt I could succeed as well."

"Do you have other things as well?" Capa asked. "Other powers?"

"There are things that I can do," Tarik answered, "that serve me well."

"Then perhaps you are indeed the man to stand up against El Muerte."

"I will be the man who stands against him," Tarik said resolutely.

For a long time neither man spoke, and then Tarik saw that Capa wept. At first he decided not to speak to him, but changed his mind. He sat closer to him and asked why he wept.

"I cannot help but weep when I think of Maria." Capa spoke each word slowly and with a nod of the head. "Only God knows how I love that fat woman. You are young, you can lose many things—your strength, your wit, your manhood. I am old and these things slipped away from me long ago. People laugh at Capa the baker, Capa the fool. The only thing I have in life is that fat woman. You know that I never liked her until I lost everything else? Now we

113

have been together so long that she has become my life. I wonder now if we will ever see her again. Even now she cries for me and wonders if I am well. She should eat something—it always makes her feel better."

"You do not worry about your own life?" Tarik asked. "You are a brave man."

"I *am* a fool. Capa the fool!" Capa spat on the ground. "Now you rest while I stand guard, and—"

Tarik looked up as the word stopped in Capa's mouth. Capa turned his head to one side and listened. From far off came the sound of hoofbeats. Tarik stood up and could see nothing. Then he mounted Zinzinbadio and looked into the distance. It was a lone rider.

"Shall we run for it?" Capa was already on his horse.

Tarik's eyes narrowed until he could discern the figure that approached them. He held up his hand for Capa to stay. He was sure that he recognized the rider who approached them. Zinzinbadio was perfectly still, while Capa's gray mare, still lathered, shifted legs uneasily, and Tarik thought that she might be sore-legged.

"It's only one?" Capa asked as the rider neared.

"One," Tarik answered.

Tarik watched as Stria drew near. She stopped her horse and dismounted. She did not speak, but squatted at the base of a tree and undid a cloth that contained cheese and bread.

"She has the same armor as you do," Capa said.

Tarik dismounted and sat by Stria. She offered the cheese and bread before her, and he took some of it.

"This bread is from my oven," Capa said. "Look, these

are the marks of my pans. Have you seen my wife? Is she safe?"

Stria sat cross-legged on the ground and ate the bread greedily. Capa watched her, not eating the bread he held in his own hands, but turning it as if he were kneading it afresh.

That day they spent each with his own thoughts, somewhat apart from one another. Tarik watched as Capa fumbled with the pans that had held the bread, and then with the loaves that had not been eaten.

But it was Stria who commanded most of Tarik's attention. She would walk away to a knoll that rose head high above the lea and stare into the distance whence they had come. They were both drawn, she and Capa, to the little town of Mentifsa—Capa because his wife was still there, Stria because she was anxious to strike the first blow. She would go to the knoll and then look toward him. Tarik groomed Zinzinbadio carefully, making sure that Stria saw him as untroubled. Tarik knew that what he had done would come to the attention of El Muerte. He saw no reason to busy himself with soldiers who came to collect the taxes from the poor.

That night they slept warily, with one and then the other taking turns watching the field stretching before them for signs of riders. None came, and the morning was a welcome sight. Capa was up early and had lost much of the melancholy of the night before. Tarik ate from the parcel of food Stria had brought and watched as Capa prepared himself for the day's adventures.

First, the round man washed one foot and then carefully

replaced his stocking and tied it below his knee. Then he put on his boot and took off the boot and the stocking of the other leg. He washed his leg and foot as carefully as he had the first and then replaced the stocking and boot.

"A man must have four friends in life," Capa said cheerfully, "two good hands to work and two good feet to carry him about. If he doesn't have these things, life will be too hard to bear. Today I have to use my feet, so I wash them carefully. If they are happy, they will carry me a long way."

"Where will they carry you?" Tarik asked.

"I have to go see about my wife," Capa said. "I will sneak back to my house and see how she fares. Maybe I will take some bread and cheese and bring her here with me—I don't know."

"And if the people see you, they will hold you for El Muerte's men!" Tarik said.

"Once a fool, twice a fool," Capa said. "What else can I do? If the only path for a man to take is a foolish path, then he has to walk like a clown."

"I will go," Stria said.

The words startled Tarik. Her voice was low and husky and came from deep within her. Capa stopped in his lacing and looked up at her. He began to tell her what she should say when she saw his wife, but the look she turned on him killed the words as they tumbled from his lips. Capa swallowed hard and turned away from her.

In a moment she was astride her horse and with a deft movement of her arm had twisted her cape about her body so that she looked again like a pile of rags on a horse.

There was a slight movement of her body, and she was off. Capa and Tarik watched as the horse galloped slowly across the field, and Tarik was reminded of the Tuareg raiders he had seen galloping their camels across the endless desert.

"Who is this girl?" Capa asked, edging closer to Tarik as he spoke. "I am not interested in you at all. A knight is a knight, even if he happens to be as black as you are. But tell me about the girl and the Crystal that allows you to see things that other men do not."

"Why do you want to know these things?" Tarik asked.

"Why?" Capa shrugged. "Why not? Fools are like babies, they stick their noses in every little place. Besides, I am happy. The girl goes to see about my wife, and I am having an adventure. How often does a baker get to have an adventure?"

"Do not be deceived," Tarik replied. "The girl goes to discover if El Muerte comes to this place—little else has meaning to her. And this adventure might still cause your death."

"Such people as you and this girl I have never seen," Capa said. "This girl is so strange."

"Stria? She presses moments of pain into her memory as some press flowers into the hands of a lover."

"And you?" Capa asked. "What pushes you, my young friend?"

"Long before I had reached the time of joining my father's nation, before I had taken the oaths of manhood and had received the markings of my people upon my body, my grandfather called me to his side." Tarik rested on one elbow. "It was on such a day as this. He told me about what had gone before, about a time when the father of my fathers had first come into the world. He climbed a great mountain, the greatest he could find, and went as high as he could until he could touch the sky itself. And when he had done this, he reached into the sky and took his share of the sky in his cupped hands and drank slowly of it, until he was filled with its spirit. When he had done this, he came down from the mountains to the banks of the river, and there he made his life.

"When he had a son, he breathed into him part of the spirit of the sky, that he might be beautiful. Part of the spirit he breathed back into the world so that it might be beautiful for his son to live in, and part of it he kept for himself." Tarik closed his eyes as he repeated the words his grandfather had spoken to him. "When his son had a son, he did this same thing—breathing part of the spirit into the son, giving part of it to the world, and keeping part of it in himself. Wherever the father went, he would be touched by the spirit of his father, and of his father's father, and it would be the same spirit.

"I am the son of the son of all sons," Tarik said, "and of the spirit of the sky as well, which dwells within me. He who wounds the spirit of my father wounds also the spirit of my son."

"I like the way you talk," Capa said. "Some of it I even understand. Now, you tell me, who is it who has wronged you?"

"You call him El Muerte."

"He doesn't count," Capa said. "A man who does everybody wrong doesn't count. Especially when he is rich and powerful. He is a way of life, like sickness. When you get sick you wait until you get better or you die. There is nothing to be done about it. You can't fight against the ground. In the end the ground wins. You like that, the way I said that?"

Tarik shrugged.

"That is the trouble with black people," Capa said, "they don't have a sense of humor."

"I did not know that you knew many black people," Tarik said. "Are there others around here?"

"You are the only one I know," Capa said.

"It's like learning about your nose from your thumb," Tarik said.

Capa changed the subject tactfully. "How did you learn to fight like that?"

"It doesn't matter," said Tarik.

"Everything matters," Capa said as he belched loudly and rubbed his belly.

TWELVE

THE SUN ROSE SLOWLY AND FILLED THE DAY WITH A hard brilliance. Tarik watched the direction from which the girl would come. He saw that Capa, too, was worried, and the thoughts of what might be happening settled heavily between them. By the time they saw a rider approaching, the day had already begun to cool and Capa had begun to wring his large hands nervously.

They saw her coming at the same time, but neither of them spoke. When she had reached them and had dismounted, Capa offered her a drink, which she did not accept.

"How do things look?" Capa asked.

The girl did not respond. She took from her horse a small carpet, which she unrolled on the ground. In the middle of the carpet was a small box.

"It is my cross," Capa said. He picked it up and opened the box for Tarik to see. Inside the box was a small cross, fashioned of polished stone. "It has been in my family for many years and is a great comfort to me. Maria knows this."

"There are soldiers coming from the north," the girl said. "The people gather silver for them and hide in their shadows."

She spat on the ground in front of Capa. Capa looked at her and then at Tarik. He gathered the stone cross and put it back into the box.

"Those are my people!" he said, standing. "They are simple people without fancy things and fancy words. When you ride away, they will still be here to work the land you spit upon. When you are gone, there will be somebody here to take his place and my people will still walk on their knees for a piece of old mutton."

"When will the soldiers come?" Tarik asked, still looking at Capa.

"They are less than a day's journey from the town," the girl answered. "Tomorrow's sun will see them here."

Tarik watched her as she took the blanket from her horse and began to rub him down. She had talked enough for one day.

"My friend"—Capa put his hand on Tarik's wrist— "forgive my impatience. When bread is baked, it rises as if every loaf would be the grandest. I am old and stale and given to crumbling around the edges—I can be forgiven. Now ask her of my wife."

"Stria?" Tarik looked toward the girl.

Stria hesitated for a moment in her rubbing, then turned and nodded her head briefly in Capa's direction.

The squat baker released the breath he had been holding and silently thanked the girl, who had already turned back to her task. Tarik watched her for a long moment and then turned his eyes to the sunset and his thoughts within.

When morning came, they saddled up early and started northward again, with Tarik leading and Stria and Capa following within a horse's length of each other. The road twisted through the low foothills and offered few vantage points from which they could see the approach of soldiers. The day was almost unbearably humid, and the shimmering heat from the sun-whitened sky blurred the shapes of the distant hills and made the very earth they traveled across seem to move before them. Tarik allowed his thoughts to drift back to the Gardens of Shange and to Nongo and Docao, wondering what would become of them. Nongo had never seen him. He wondered what image the old man carried in his head.

"Haloo!" It was Capa.

Tarik turned and saw Capa pointing ahead of them to the left. They were crossing a small field in one of the few open places along the road. Tarik shielded his eyes from the sun and peered ahead. There were riders, three, perhaps four. They carried a standard and rode at a good pace.

"They could be soldiers," Capa said, pulling alongside Tarik. "Shall we go off the road?"

"No, it is too late," Tarik said. "If we see them, they can see us as well. Take Stria and wait in that stand. If they see me alone and they are knights, they will undoubtedly try me singly."

Capa turned and signaled Stria to the side of the road

and into the stand. Tarik took Zinzinbadio to a wide spot in the road where the ground was firmer than in the surrounding field. He sat still on the great horse and waited, checking the position of the sun as he did so, so that he could keep his back to it.

The approaching knights slowed and then stopped when they saw that Tarik waited for them. Zinzinbadio threw his head back and shook it impatiently. The four knights were dressed in heavy untanned leather tunics and wore no helmets. Three were identical in every aspect of dress, while the fourth had a small cloak of feathers around his shoulders, and feathers ringed the top of his boots.

They drew their horses so that the heads of the horses were together. Then one of them turned and started slowly toward Tarik. When he had covered half the distance between them, the strange knight drew his sword and Tarik did the same.

"Lay down your sword, dog." The knight spoke with contempt. "I am in the service of the Prince."

"Your only service this day," Tarik responded, "is to the arms of death."

The knight's lips parted in what, in a less gruesome face, might have been construed as a smile.

"What is this moment of night that is so eager to fall? Let us hear if you die with a scream on your lips or a sob."

Tarik did not see the knight signal his horse, but suddenly the knight was upon him, bringing his sword straight for Tarik's breast. Zinzinbadio wheeled sideways as Tarik's sword caught that of the strange knight and forced it aside. The knight's horse wheeled back toward

123

Zinzinbadio and charged again. Again Tarik parried. In a few moments Serq found its mark and the knight was dead.

The next knight to challenge Tarik was the one with the feathered cloak. Tarik imagined him to be the leader of this small band and prepared himself for the onslaught. The feathered knight wielded a two-headed ax, swinging it above his head as he came slowly toward Tarik, clucking to his horse as he did so. It was a large horse, as large as Zinzinbadio but broader. It was not the kind of horse one used for speed, but for sturdiness in battle. Tarik waited until the last moment and then, timing his charge, rushed toward the oncoming knight. Tarik's sword collided with the feathered knight's swinging ax high over their heads and sent a shower of sparks down around them. The force of the blow sent shivers up Tarik's arms, but Serq did not drop from his hand. The feathered knight took his horse past Tarik and stopped. He turned and slowly unlaced the sides of his armor. The man's arms were as huge as the mid-limbs of an oak, with great bulging veins that went over the curves of the huge muscles like a twisting river. He nudged his horse and again came at Tarik. His horse stopped with its head next to Zinzinbadio's, and the feathered knight swung his ax again and again, each blow crashing toward Tarik's neck and shoulders and coming with all the fury of an eagle beating its wings against the raging storm. Tarik warded off the blows as they came. He knew that the large ax was heavier than his sword and would soon tire even those great arms.

But suddenly Zinzinbadio swung around and began to

back toward the side of the mountain. Tarik tried to straighten him again but could not. Then Tarik saw the reason for the great horse's movement: one of the other knights was galloping quickly toward him. Tarik stopped Zinzinbadio's backstepping and feinted toward the feathered knight. Then, swinging his body low alongside his horse's neck, Tarik spurred the animal into the path of the galloping knight. As he thrust Serq upward through the neck of the startled horseman, he felt the handle of the feathered knight's battle-ax glance against his shoulder. But the knight Tarik had struck clutched his throat and fell, mortally wounded, to the dusty road. There were now only the two against Tarik.

Tarik did not wait for the last knight to charge. He urged Zinzinbadio toward the stationary horseman and caught him trying to remove his bow from his back. Tarik's sword whistled through the air and cut deeply into the lean shoulder.

Now Tarik turned his attention once again to the feathered knight. He braced himself as the knight charged and easily warded off a wild swing of the huge ax. But as Tarik started to deliver his own blow, the feathered giant released his ax and, grabbing Tarik's wrist with one hand, delivered a crashing blow with his free hand that sent Tarik's senses reeling. For a moment Tarik was confused, and then he saw the glint of the sun against the blade of the feathered knight's ax high above his head. Tarik lunged out of the way of the ax as it arched downward. He felt himself falling from Zinzinbadio's back and slammed hard onto the ground.

The feathered knight cursed as his horse reared high above Tarik. Tarik sprang to his feet and leaped under the horse to avoid the plummeting ax, coming up from the rear side and running Serq blindly over his head toward the still-mounted knight. The weight of the horse came crashing down, its sweated flank sending Tarik again to the hard earth. And then another weight, seemingly as great as that of the horse which now stood above him, fell heavily by his side. It was the feathered knight, who landed in a heap beside Tarik. Tarik grasped the handle of Serq with both hands and plunged it into the knight as he tried to regain his feet.

Tarik saw that the feathered knight was dead. He looked around him and saw that the knight whose shoulder he had wounded now staggered toward him, a dagger in his good hand. Tarik rose to one knee and tried to pull his sword from the feathered knight, but it would not budge. Tarik braced himself and wrenched again at the sword that was buried in the bosom of his adversary, but again to no avail. Then there was the sudden sound of hoofbeats. Tarik turned just in time to see Stria pull her horse to a cruel stop and leap from it onto the last remaining knight. Tarik was on his knees, his head still spinning from the blow the feathered knight had dealt him. The girl was accounting herself well against the knight, and by the time that Tarik had finally pried his sword from its grisly container, she had finished her opponent.

Now it was Capa who rode up to them and announced that there were more riders coming.

"Foot soldiers!" he announced.

Tarik tried to stand and felt his legs give way beneath him. Capa lifted him to Zinzinbadio's back and, once Stria had mounted, they rode back to the small camp they had made for themselves the night before. Tarik lay down on a bed of leaves and fell asleep.

He awoke with a start and saw that the sky was black and stained. His head still ached, and when he tried to sit up, the pain in his leg made him wince. There was a sound of footsteps, and he turned to see Stria coming toward him.

"Where is Capa?" Tarik asked.

She did not answer but knelt by his side. He had been wounded just above the knee, and his stocking was caked with mud and his own blood. She poured some of the wine that she had brought from town and poured it on the wound. Then she carefully lifted the cloth away from the wound and tore an opening in the stocking with her teeth. Tarik looked at the wound and saw that it was not deep but that his leg was swollen. The girl looked at it carefully, then cut a thin slice of bread and placed it directly on the wound. After this she placed several large leaves over it and tied it onto the leg with a thin vine binding.

"You know many useful things," Tarik said.

Stria looked at him for a long moment, as if his words had brought something to mind, and then she began to eat the rest of the bread. Tarik sat up and supported his weight on a blanket. His head was still not completely clear. There was a great deal of blood on his clothing that he knew had not come from his own wound. There was blood on Stria as well, and he remembered how she had attacked the last knight.

His victory had brought him no joy. The reasons for winning his battles, reasons once firm, now eddied so tenuously between his quest and the deaths he had caused that he could hold them in neither the palm nor the heart, but only in awkward postures unfit for dreams or legends. Nongo had warned him of the power of Evil but had not warned him that the face of Right could be as strange. Yet what of his father and of his brothers and of their spirits cut down before his eyes?

Tarik shivered. His mouth was dry.

He closed his eyes and thought again of all that had happened that day and wondered, if he had clearly seen the end before the challenge, what the ending would have been. And somewhere within him, away from heart and brain, the thought occurred to him that he would either kill again or leave this land at once. Either way, Tarik would not be the child his mother knew.

"How easy this killing business becomes," Tarik said. "Once it can be done when the heart is angry, it comes as a child to its mother. Is this the gift that Nongo and Docao have given me?"

"It is a gift to do what has to be done," Stria said. She was twisting strips of leather into a wide band. Her fingers moved deftly, pulling each strip of leather, before tightening the weave, to see if it would stretch.

" 'The words come easy," Tarik said. " 'This is Evil and this is Good.' Choosing which is which comes hard."

Stria came to Tarik with the finished band. She put it

128

around his leg where he had been wounded, and tied the ends.

"As you slept I put my ear to your chest, listening for the beating of your heart. I prayed to hear it because you are Good." Stria tied the leather band around Tarik's leg, testing it with her fingers to see that it was not too tight. "Your heart beats and mine beats and we live. Between the beats, in the silences, we make our choices. We choose or die. What is your choice, black friend?"

"To do the thing that must be done," Tarik answered.

The girl looked at him and for the first time she smiled. Her teeth were small and white, and her smile filled her face and made her appear younger. But it was not a smile of warmth, but of a delight that Tarik realized he did not share, and that sent a cold chill over his body.

ThIRTEEN

CAPA RETURNED AT DAYBREAK AND AS USUAL WAS excited.

"Where have you been?" Tarik asked.

"Where have I been?" Capa looked toward Stria. "Didn't she . . . ? Of course she didn't. I went back to the village to see what was what."

"And?"

"Do you know the knight who wore the cape of eagles?" Capa asked.

"The feathers around his shoulders?"

"Yes, the very one," Capa said. "He was none other than a cousin of El Muerte himself! Now all the people talk about what has happened. With one eye they look around for El Muerte and with the other they look around for you. Some say that you are greater than El Muerte himself and will save the town. Others say that you will be angry because they have betrayed you and that you will seek revenge."

"So it was El Muerte's cousin." Tarik closed his eyes.

"Did you know, Capa, that I had a brother who was killed
in this wild place?"

"What do I know of you?" Capa said. "You come here
like someone who casts stones with the devil. You are a
boy and yet you are a man. I don't know anything about
you. The more I see, the less I know. And this one who
comes with you is just as strange."

"I had a brother and he was called Umeme," Tarik said.
"He was as full of color as a ripe berry. When he was little
I would say to him, 'Umeme, when will you become a
person? You look like a berry and walk like a wild hen.'
And do you know what else he did, Capa?"

"What else?"

"He would laugh in his sleep," Tarik said. "When he
did this, our mother would say that the spirits were play-
ing with him in his dreams."

"That's nice," Capa said.

Tarik could see that Capa was already half asleep, and
he closed his own eyes and thought of the times when he
and Umeme used to throw stones along the water's edge
and annoy the Kikuyu fishermen. With these pleasant
thoughts, he drifted off to sleep and began to dream.

The dream at first was quite pleasant. He dreamed of
walking along a long strip of red earth. As he walked, the
day grew warmer and then colder and then warmer again.
There was nothing that he could do to make himself at
ease. Then, with his mind in this concern, he suddenly
heard a low voice, almost a growl. He turned to see what
looked like a Tuareg woman. Her face was half hidden in
her veils, and only the blue markings across her forehead

could be seen. She was at once woman and hyena and came toward him slowly. He tried to move away but could not think of where to go, only that he was getting colder.

When he awoke again, he felt himself shivering. There were arms around him and a fire burned an arm's length from him. "Ho, he wakes," he heard Capa say, "maybe the fever breaks now."

It was the girl's arms around him. She was on the side of him away from the fire, giving him the heat of her body as she held him closely to her. He was still shivering, but even so the sweat began to pour from his forehead. He tried to speak but found his lips and throat were dry. The girl put her fingers to his lips.

"Sleep," she said. "There is nothing else to be done."

It was almost the voice of an old woman, and Tarik knew that it was the growling that he had heard in his dream.

"Sleep," she said again.

She had her shawl around her shoulders, and now she moved it and pulled his face so that it lay against her flesh, and then she pulled the shawl around both of them. Now her entire body was wrapped around Tarik's. She spoke softly; sometimes he could understand what she was saying and sometimes he could not.

"The fire burns," she said. "There is darkness in the flames and light as well. There is life in the flames and dancing . . . sometimes one and then the other. You have only to sleep, and I will watch . . . all will be well . . . all will be well."

The words seemed further and further away, coming

softly and quickly disappearing, leaving warm traces of comfort at the edges of his mind like water disappearing on black skin beneath a high sun. Tarik closed his eyes to a dark, uneasy peace.

The sun was already high when Tarik woke. The swelling in his leg had gone down, and although he did not feel as strong as he thought he might, he knew he was ready to begin his quest again.

"Glad to have you back among the living, my friend!" Capa said. "For a while there I wasn't sure which way you were headed."

Tarik looked around and saw the girl sitting against a tree.

"It is good to have friends to take care of you," he said to her. She looked away from him.

"There was a lad I knew tending his goats," Capa said. "I spoke to him and asked him what was going on in the town. He said there are soldiers everywhere, and it is rumored that El Muerte himself is coming to find you. One of the knights you fought lived long enough to speak of you before he died. Now they say that El Muerte seeks you."

"He will find me," Tarik said.

"Not here, I hope," Capa answered. "If he finds you here when his soldiers are with him, there will be no escaping him. The best you could hope for is to kill him as he or his men try to kill you. I think you should move on and make him hunt you."

"Here!" The girl spoke. "If he wants to come here,

then we should wait for him here!"

"She is not a clever girl," Capa said, biting into an apple. "She is ferocious with that thing dangling around her neck like the cross of St. Andrew, but she is not a wise person."

The girl spat between Capa and Tarik.

"My purpose is to find him," Tarik said. "Then to deal with him."

"That is a good purpose," Capa said. "I would like nothing more than to see you find him . . . to see the two of you find him. Two ferocious children that you are—"

"I am not a child," Tarik said. "Don't let your eyes deceive you, Capa."

"I am wrong, of course," Capa said. "It is my thinking that only children could have passions so great for a mission and so little for life. And what beautiful children! You with your strong black face and gentle eyes. As for the girl, how can she be so intense a creature with her little round face at such a tender age? Neither of you have lived long enough to be truly in love with living. Believe me, it is a good thing. Consider this, when have you heard anyone say that death is better than life? I mean anyone who has died and knows what he is talking about? No, living is a good thing. El Muerte knows this. Poof! He will send his soldiers to do his work for him and then bring the pieces of your body for his hawk to feed upon. Did you think he would leap to face you, knowing that you have already dispatched his cousin and three of his best knights?"

"One was mine!" the girl said.

"I am reminded." Capa shuddered. "Still, he knows that it is a formidable opponent he has encountered."

"I will go on," Tarik said. "And look for him in another place."

"It is the wisdom of a man who will one day have a fat wife to love," Capa said.

Tarik smiled and asked Capa to gather their belongings together. When Capa had agreed to this and had begun, Tarik went to speak to Stria.

"I do not think it wise for you to come with us," Tarik said. "What Capa said was right. You do not fear death, you invite it. It is something that Nongo and Docao saw in your eyes also."

"Men see what they want in the eyes of a woman," the girl said, her voice like distant thunder. "If I had not come along, your body would be feeding maggots this day."

"I am thankful," Tarik answered. "You have given me my life, and now I wish to offer you the chance not to risk yours."

"Be about yourself, black one," she said, "and I will be about mine."

Tarik watched as Stria turned her attention to her horse, checking each hoof carefully for small stones. He wanted to tell her that he had looked into the Crystal again and had seen an image of himself lying on the ground with El Muerte above him. He had closed his eyes for a moment, and when he opened them the image had disappeared. He stood and went into the high grass to relieve himself.

After Capa finished gathering their stuff, Tarik mounted Zinzinbadio and nudged the horse. Capa followed at his heels. When they had gone for a while, Tarik turned back and saw a horse going slowly along the path that he and Capa had traveled. On the horse there was a rider wrapped in a gray shawl, and Tarik was pleased.

Tarik, seeing that Stria was determined to travel with them, bade Capa wait for her, and when she had reached them and they had exchanged greetings, Tarik said that it would be best for them to travel together. This the girl agreed to, and together they traveled westward toward Lauro.

It was possible, as they traveled, to trace the movements of El Muerte and his men, for wherever he traveled, people fled from his path, and of those who did not flee, many were killed or maimed. Thus it was that when they reached the outskirts of Lauro they met pilgrims fleeing from that village heading to the provinces of Madrid.

They came upon a merchant who was fleeing with his two daughters, and Capa asked him if it was indeed true that El Muerte was in the town of Lauro, and how many men were with him.

"He is there with at least a dozen knights and a hundred soldiers," the merchant said. "They search the city, looking for one they call the Magician."

"The Magician?" Capa looked at the merchant and wondered what was meant. "Does he describe this magician fellow?"

"Yes," the merchant replied. "He is as black as night and from deep in the heart of Alkebu-lan. They say that only El Muerte can defeat him in battle. That is because he does not fight with skill but with magic. He befuddles the mind with his sorcery."

"Poof!" Capa said. "He does no such thing. He is simply a marvelous fighter with unbelievable courage."

"Say what you will," said the merchant, "but such a man has great power, and power is always evil."

"You are old, my friend," Capa said in return, "but still as ignorant as the day you were born. Never fear, ignorance is the best tonic for sleep. What else does this evil man say? Does he say which way he will travel next?"

"Why are you so interested in the whereabouts of El Muerte?" the merchant asked warily. "Such information is not to be taken lightly."

"Always the merchant, eh?" Capa replied. "But tell me what you know."

"Tell me first why you want to know it," said the merchant, releasing the grip on his younger daughter's hand and pulling his garment at the knee for comfort.

"Well, it is obvious," Capa said. "I am thinking of following El Muerte and picking his pocket. If I know where he goes, I can do this thing."

"Do you believe me such a fool as to swallow the likes of that?" The merchant sneered. "You would sooner pluck out your own eyes than offend such a man as El Muerte!"

"On the other hand," continued Capa, withdrawing his dagger from its sheath. "I could do just as well by cutting your scrawny throat and taking your gold. Which of my stories do you believe, my friend?"

The merchant looked at Capa with alarm, then with

137

disbelief, and then with alarm again as the round baker ran his tongue along the edge of his dagger.

"He has taken two prisoners," the merchant said finally, "a priest from the south and a blind man. I have seen these two and know by the talk that is bandied about that they must have something to do with the magician that El Muerte seeks. This is confirmed even more by the ebony color of the blind man. He takes them to Olcades, where he will deal with them.

"Now I must be on my way so that I reach my destination by nightfall," the merchant said, still looking at Capa's dagger. Capa smiled and pinched one of the merchant's daughters on her ample cheek and then watched them ride off in their little carriage.

When Capa came back to their camp and told Tarik what the merchant had told him, he was surprised to see how upset Tarik was.

"I don't understand," Capa said. "Are you indeed a magician? You have wondrous things about you. Are the priests of your faith?"

"They are priests of vengeance," Tarik said, "and that is my faith as well. We must go to Olcades."

"It could be a trap," Capa said. "El Muerte is not the fool that Capa is. If this merchant learns something of El Muerte, it is because El Muerte wishes it to be learned."

"And if he learns something of me," Tarik said, "it will be because I wish him to learn. But we must go to Olcades. I owe these men each breath I take. If I can rescue them it is my duty to do so."

"And if it is a trap?" Capa asked, warily.

"I haven't come this far to turn away from danger," Tarik answered. "When I was left for dead by El Muerte and was brought back to life by the two men he has now captured, I grew to love them the way that one loves two fathers. They have taught me, and made me stronger than I was. I cannot follow my father's steps into manhood, but they have given me another way."

"I think you've had too much of this holy mission business," Capa said, sucking on the end of a piece of fresh cane. "It goes to your head like young mead."

"I wondered what made my knees tremble so," Tarik responded, smiling. "At any rate, even if you are right, what do you have better to offer as comfort for my journey?"

Capa shrugged, and continued sucking on the cane.

The trip to Olcades was an arduous one. Capa's horse grew lame as they passed Idubeda, and he had to stop and buy a new one. It took them two full days to find a new animal for Capa, but Tarik thought it wise to have a sound steed. They spent a day resting before they went on the road that entered the city. When they reached the road, it was Capa's idea that they disguise themselves.

"We could disguise ourselves as merchants or priests," Capa said. "I remember once when my wife and I were traveling to New Carthage for the sun, we traveled as priest and nun. That way we were not robbed."

"Cowards hide from danger," Tarik answered.

"Cowards?" Capa looked at Tarik. "Did I not tell you

that my father was a coward? And his father before him? If I am indeed a coward it is a great relief, for I thought surely I had been come by poorly."

As they neared the city, they saw many people hurrying along the road, many carrying goats or sucklings and some with pots of cheese or skins of wine.

"Why are these people hurrying to this city?" Tarik asked. "I thought people fled from El Muerte, not into his embrace."

Capa shrugged. He talked to some of the people. Then he returned to Tarik to say that there would be games and contests that day and that El Muerte himself would duel a young knight.

"What kind of life do these people hold who would celebrate with such as this man?" Tarik sneered at those who scurried along the road.

"Even lobsters dance when they are not in the pot," Capa said.

As they neared Olcades, the roadsides began to fill with merchants selling wares, as well as beggars, acrobats, minstrels, and holy men of various sects. The acrobats were especially fascinating to Tarik, some of the teams balancing as many as four of their number on their shoulders. Musicians in bright costumes played flutes, shawms, and cymbals; veiled dark women sold elaborately carved oranges and lemons, while the discarded rinds lay about their feet like gaily painted snake skins.

There were several black men with pinched Berber features who sold cooked slivers of lamb glazed with an almost clear mint. Tarik watched as one carved a piece of meat with an incredibly sharp ivory-handled kris, twisted it deftly between long fingers, and skewered it onto a stick. Then he took a lemon and squeezed it the length of the meat before dipping it quickly in and out of the mint glaze.

Tarik found his thoughts drifting back to the time when he had run at his father's heels in the marketplace at Timbuktu and had been frightened by the chanting white-robed students of the ulama to whom his father gave cowrie shells.

"It will be wise to stop here," Tarik said. "These peddlers will know everything that goes on in Olcades."

A quick movement by Stria caught his attention, and he watched her make her way through the crowd where a group of women busied themselves setting out pots and colored puffs of cotton, the kind that women gave to their children to play with in Jenne. Stria pushed herself among the women roughly, spoke to them, and then left them to come to his side.

"What people are those?" Tarik asked.

"Gitano," the girl replied.

"Are they your people?"

"They say that there are spies along the road and that they are looking for a black knight on a black horse."

"Let me talk to the people," Capa said. "I will see what I can discover. Even strangers talk to me freely."

Tarik agreed to this and took Zinzinbadio onto a small crest that overlooked the road. Stria went with him, but instead of dismounting as Tarik did, she stood on her horse and pulled herself up into the branches of a tree.

141

Here, half concealed by the leaves, she, too, watched the road below.

Tarik found himself angered by his wait, but quickly fought off his impatience. He tried to think why he was angry, and wondered if the training that he had received was beginning to wear thin. But no, he thought, it was a different kind of anger than he had felt—that he still felt—for El Muerte. It was the kind of anger he had felt once when he had sat outside a council house waiting for his father. His father had been a long time in the council house, speaking with the elders on some matter, and Tarik had grown weary of waiting. When finally his father had come from the meeting and they had started the long trek home, Tarik had begun to tell his father about the shape of a boat he had seen in the clouds, but his father had silenced him with a wave of the hand, and they had walked home in silence, the father with his long strides, lost in his thoughts, and Tarik, scampering to keep up, angered at his father's refusal to allow him to talk to him, a right that Tarik had thought his after the long wait.

Yet it was not exactly the waiting that angered Tarik. When he looked up into the tree and saw Stria, perched motionlessly in the branches, he realized the cause of his anger. He wanted to go down to the road, to mingle with the peddlers, to join the festivities. He wished even more to get on with those things he had begun what now seemed ages ago. Even the long haggling over which merchant would have his wares in the sun, where the colors would seem more brilliant, now touched his memory warmly. The deaths of his family had taken a large piece of his life away, and avenging those deaths took still more.

A stirring above him startled him as Stria dropped easily down on her horse. Before Tarik could speak, she had ridden away. Tarik walked to the top of the crest and looked at the road below, but saw nothing amiss. He climbed into the tree where Stria had been and again peered down at the road. The colors, from where he sat, were clear spots of red, green, blue, black, yellow, and dazzling whites. Now and again a section would find the colors coming together as people strolled in groups or acrobats flung themselves about, and then the colors would seem to merge and form new hues, only to separate again.

He could see Stria. She rode slowly along the far side of the road, stopping to speak with the women she had first questioned, and then, wheeling her animal sharply across the road, she returned toward the crest. Tarik watched her ride, her bare legs hardly moving along the horse's withers as she rode far forward on its back.

"Why did you go to the road?" Tarik asked. Stria had stopped directly beneath him and pulled herself easily into the tree.

"Two soldiers have Capa," she said huskily. "There!"

Tarik looked to where Stria pointed. He saw the two soldiers standing on either side of Capa. The baker turned from one to the other, gesticulating with his hands. A third soldier approached, and soon Capa was speaking with him as well.

"I have to get him," Tarik said. "These soldiers will kill him for the sport."

143

"No," Stria said. "There are too many of them for now. Let him be taken."

"I wouldn't leave a dog to their clutches," Tarik said, dropping from the tree.

"No." Stria dropped to the ground in front of Tarik. "Leave him be. I have spoken to some who will not allow him to be taken."

"Those women?" Tarik started to mount Zinzinbadio. "You think the soldiers would not kill them?"

He had one foot in the stirrup and had just lifted the other to swing over Zinzinbadio's back when he felt Stria's arm around his throat. She twisted his head and threw him heavily to the ground. Tarik shook his head and looked up at the girl, who stood over him.

"Leave him be," Stria said. "He cannot kill El Muerte."

Tarik rolled over backward and sprung to his feet. Stria stood before him, her legs spread and bent at the knees, waiting for him. The dagger she wore around her neck she now held before her.

Tarik looked at her, then leaped forward, grabbing for the wrist of the hand that held the dagger. He got it and twisted her wrist as hard as he could toward the ground.

For a long moment Stria matched him strength for strength, and when it seemed that he would finally overcome her, she let him push her right hand onto the ground while she pushed his shoulder backward with her other hand. Again Tarik fell heavily on the ground, this time with Stria on him. Tarik twisted violently, throwing her off, and tried to get to his feet. Stria was quickly on his back. He threw her off again, somehow managing to get

144

to his feet. She stood facing him again, her body low, her arms and legs apart. Tarik knew that he could not stop her attacks without injuring her. Her strength seemed to come from her legs, and he thought of kicking them out from under her. He circled once to the left, then quickly to the right, and was about to attack her when she suddenly stood up and relaxed.

"Listen," she said.

There was an eerie sound coming from the direction of the road. Stria walked by Tarik to the top of the crest and looked down. Tarik followed and also looked to see where the sound came from.

On the road below, the women to whom Stria had been speaking stood at the side of the road in a half circle. Others alongside the road watched them as they made the wailing noise that Tarik had heard. On the road the three soldiers, Capa between them, were moving toward the stone gateway into Olcades. The women took off their shawls and began twirling them in the air, and then, in a body, flung themselves at the soldiers. The twirling shawls went into the faces of the soldiers, who were soon enveloped completely by the women.

Stria moved quickly to her horse and rode down the crest at a breakneck speed, whipping and slashing the horse with a fury. The horse nearly crashed headlong into the women, who, some still making the eerie wailing noise, now surrounded Capa and the soldiers.

Tarik watched as Stria pulled Capa onto her horse and started back toward the crest.

When she returned, the horse was badly lathered and

wild-eyed and shook with coughing from its efforts. She leaped quickly from the animal and began to walk it about.

Tarik looked down at the road. The women had disap-peared. The soldiers lay in the road, still.

Tarik looked at Stria's horse. The animal was still suf-fering from its exertion. He looked at Stria questioningly.

"The women would have killed Capa as well," she said, still walking the horse slowly about.

"You do not know that," Tarik said.

"It is what I told them to do in case the soldiers lived to tell of our plans," Stria said. "But if you care so much . . ."

They rested until nearly nightfall and then decided to enter Olcades. Tarik would draw the soldiers' attention. Capa and Stria would enter the city, and Tarik would find them later. It was Capa's idea to find the home of a baker in which to stay.

Most of the roadside venders had left, but there were still a few who displayed their wares near the gates. While Capa and Stria held their horses among trees off the road, Tarik rode slowly toward the gate. He saw more people just inside the gate. He stopped and watched them for a while. He saw that their eyes would turn toward the inner walls of the gate, even when their heads would not, and sensed that soldiers crouched just beyond the wall.

Then he turned Zinzinbadio around and started gallop-ing slowly away from the city. No sooner had he done so than he heard a shout from behind him. He turned and saw soldiers running from the walls, and then galloping horsemen. He let them draw close before he patted Zinzinbadio's neck.

The huge horse increased the length of his stride slowly as he moved away from the wall. The horsemen who followed rode swiftly but were no match. They slashed at their horses until the poor beasts lathered at their mouths in a vain effort to keep up with Zinzinbadio. When they saw how effortlessly Tarik had left them in the dust of the road, they thought that he had somehow bewitched their horses into not running, and this is what they told El Muerte when they returned.

FOURTEEN

IN HIS PALACE EL MUERTE SAT EATING GOOSE WITH A
silver dagger as he listened to the report of one of his
soldiers.

"Sire, the black one waved his hand like so," the horsemen said, "and stilled the legs of our steeds. We whipped
them until blood was drawn but could come no closer than
the black one desired."

"Do they speak the truth?" El Muerte turned his gaze
upon Jad the Unclean.

"They speak the truth, master," Jad said. "The black
one we have captured and the other are magicians as well.
If they seem lifeless, it is because they have willed their
essence to this one while they are still alive!"

"What is this you say? Give a meaning to it."

"They have turned over their souls to Satan, who has
replaced it with an essence that gives them great power.
This essence they have willed to this black knight so that
he may defeat you, master."

"Can this be done?" El Muerte asked, throwing a bone

148

to Jad. "Can this fool stand against me?"

El Muerte watched as Jad eagerly sucked the bone. El Muerte knew that it would be useless to try to hurry his answer without resorting to a whip. When the small creature had finished sucking the bone clean and licking his fingers, he answered.

"No mere man stands against El Muerte, master." Jad nodded to himself. "But if he does not stand before you, if he creeps in the night like the shadow of the moon, then he is dangerous."

"He knows I have his familiars locked in my dungeon, and he plans his course from there," El Muerte said. "I will hurry his plans so that they are less perfect."

El Muerte probed the innards of the goose for more meat with the tip of his dagger. When he saw that the bones were bare, he kicked the carcass away from him.

"Bring me the one with one hand," he said to the horseman who had told him of Tarik's deeds.

The horseman brought him Docao and put him before El Muerte.

"How did you lose your hand, pig?" El Muerte asked.

Docao did not reply. It was Jad who told his master how Docao had lost his hand. El Muerte roared with laughter until his face reddened and his eyes watered.

"I cut your hand off for defying me and you fight with the stump?" El Muerte asked. "This is a thing that should be talked about a great deal and told again! Isn't this so, Jad?"

"Yes, master," Jad answered.

"Yes, talk about it!"

149

"It is an odd thing," Jad said, "that a man loses his hand and then fights on against the very one who has relieved him of his hand in the first place. It is a strange thing indeed!"

"But it is a thing that makes my blood boil!" screamed El Muerte.

"His very blood boils!" echoed Jad.

El Muerte glared at Docao. "How wicked of you to defy the mercy I have shown you in not killing you when I first laid eyes on your miserable carcass!"

"What insolence!" said Jad.

"Pray for mercy," El Muerte commanded Docao.

"I pray only to my God for His holy mercy!" Docao answered.

El Muerte asked for a sword, and the horseman who had brought Docao from his dungeon gave El Muerte his sword. With one swing El Muerte severed the head of the priest Docao. Then with a second swing he severed the head of the horseman who had failed to catch Tarik.

By this time the slaves of El Muerte had brought in the roast lamb and El Muerte dined on this as Jad hovered near his shoulder, waiting for pieces of succulent flesh.

FIFTEEN

OLCADES BRISTLED WITH NERVOUS ACTIVITY. TARIK, WEARing a monk's robe fashioned for him by Capa, mingled with the crowds and learned as much as he could from the snatches of conversation he overheard. The games were to last for two days. The first day there would be contests between groups of nine and seven men, and the following day there would be contests of single combatants.

There was much talk as well about the death of El Muerte's cousin, and of the knight who had killed him. Each story that Tarik heard was more fantastic than the last. One story had it that the knight who had attacked El Muerte's cousin had swept down from the heavens in the shape of a bird, and another that two arrows had pierced his heart without effect. But it was clear to Tarik that El Muerte knew of him and thought him to be somewhere near Olcades and hoped to draw him out.

Soldiers mingled with the crowds, and Tarik was careful to avoid them. Once the games began, the soldiers paid

151

less attention to the crowd that milled uneasily in the town square.

The first contest was between seven of El Muerte's soldiers and seven slaves they had brought with them. They looked, to Tarik, like the Greek traders he had once seen in Jenne. Tarik soon saw also how El Muerte would run the games, for while his soldiers wore both shields and swords, the slaves were allowed only one small stick with which to defend their lives.

There was a clearing made, and El Muerte's soldiers formed a large ring. The crowd pressed in on them, eager to gain good viewing spots. The slaves were led in, and then the soldiers followed, to the cheers of the crowd. There was a spot in the circle left open, and it was there that a wagon, drawn by two handsome white horses, came to a stop. On the wagon there was a tent that bore the image of a large bird with wings outstretched. The side of the tent was lifted, and there, sitting on an enormous stack of pillows, was El Muerte. At his side, looking very much like a wild animal shorn of its fur to the flesh, sat the hunched and grinning Jad the Unclean.

El Muerte lifted his hand, and the slaves were untied. They were given the sticks and at once were surrounded by the soldiers. The slaves fought bravely but were no match with their sticks against the cutting edges of the soldiers' swords, and they were soon vanquished.

Another group was quickly brought forth, and the killing continued. El Muerte himself participated, his grin hideously cracking his face, his hair matted against his sweating brow, his huge arms swinging his sword almost sensuously through the still air. To Tarik, it was as if El Muerte were reaching out to the people of the village, not with his senses, but with his evilness, knowing that it was only in their horror that he touched them.

The soldiers roared their approval at each killing and began to urge the townspeople to do likewise. The faint cheers from the shocked townspeople of Olcades cracked in their throats like the rattle of death in the damp air.

Tarik had seen El Muerte before, had seen him kill his father, but even so the skill of the man and his great strength were wondrous to behold.

"Hear ye! Hear ye!" One of the soldiers stood a few feet from El Muerte. "Tomorrow there will be more contests, and music which all will enjoy. Whoever fights bravely and wins will get five pieces of gold. Whoever fights him in whose shadow I stand and wins will get his weight in gold!"

"Heeee!" Jad the Unclean screeched.

It was enough. For the first time Tarik could feel the presence of El Muerte in his bowels. It grew heavy and rumbled and made his legs tremble and the palms of his hands sweat for wanting to feel the handle of his own sword.

That evening he inquired of several children where he might find bread and was told to go to the house of Pen, the baker. Tarik waited until night had fallen before he went there.

The door opened slowly, and one shiny eye peered out.

Then the door opened farther and Capa pulled Tarik into the house. When this was done, a lamp of oil was lit and Tarik saw Capa and the baker, Pen.

"All the town is frightened," Capa said. "The men who were killed were well loved."

"Then why do they not stand against this beast?" Tarik said.

"Because it promises to end tomorrow." Capa shrugged. "Each man thinks that he will be spared."

Tarik asked about Stria, and Capa nodded toward the corner, where the girl sat, one knee supporting her chin, her eyes closed.

"She sleeps?" Tarik asked.

"Who knows what she does?" Capa answered. "It is enough to know that what I thought was true was true. The baker Pen tells me that El Muerte had visited a local poisoner and bought many potions. He burns these potions in incense holders day and night to confound his enemies. He means to meet you here and destroy you."

"You are the one he seeks?" Pen pointed a stubby finger at Tarik.

"This is the knight who will defeat the dog out there," Capa said.

"He will kill you," Pen said. As he spoke, he patted his arm with his fingers as if he were trying to arouse himself from dozing. "He will split you in half like a chicken and feed you to his dogs!"

"You don't know what you are talking about!" Capa said with great disgust. "How can you be so stupid and still be a baker?"

154

"He will kill you," Pen said. "He is too powerful. His soldiers will drag you about the square by your tongue and you will forget your mother's name. Best you run now before you leave your stench on my floor and cause my death as well!"

"Shut up, old fool," Capa said. "I've already paid for our lodging tonight and I will keep both eyes on you until the cock crows. Your belly was another color when you took my gold."

"You said he was a great man, a terror!" Pen said. "He doesn't look like much of a terror to me."

"If your tongue knew of this man's powers, it would strangle you for uttering such a blasphemy!" Capa's face reddened. "Would it help if he shed some innocent blood? Would you dance then?"

"We will see," said Pen, "what we will see!"

With that, Pen took his blanket and went to a corner to sleep.

"Can he be trusted?" Tarik asked, watching Pen curl into a tight knot in his corner.

"No," Capa said, "but he can be watched, which is even better when one deals with sheep. But Pen is not our problem. El Muerte is our problem. Anyone can see how he baits his trap with the deaths of these innocents to draw you out."

"I am ready to spring his trap for him," Tarik said.

"It is an impossible thing with all his soldiers around him," Capa said. "He does not relieve himself of their presence for a moment. He believes what he has heard of you and is wary."

155

"My friends are here," Tarik answered. "I cannot abandon them."

"They say that he has already killed one of them." Capa put his hand on Tarik's shoulder. "The one who had but one hand."

"Docao? He has killed Docao?"

"Tarik, look at me." Capa stood before Tarik. "I am not as great as you, but my heart is good. I tell you that El Muerte has taken the life, but only you can make your friend's death a vain thing. He invested his life in this struggle he believed in. Now you must deny your heart and use your head."

"You must use your sword." The low voice of Stria filled the room. "Or I will use mine!"

"Dear God, the girl will get us all killed," Capa said. "She wants to die. She doesn't care." Capa turned to Stria. "If you want to become a saint, it is your business. I myself am not yet ready to be worshipped. I want nothing more from life than to die a hideously old man. Is this too much to ask?"

Tarik turned toward Stria and looked at her intently. She had drawn her shawl around her so that only her eyes and dark hair were visible.

"Stria." Tarik spoke quietly. "I ask only that you let me strike first."

Stria spat on the floor and turned away.

"I wish my fat wife were here," Capa said. "This could very well be my last night on this earth."

The next day the soldiers went from house to house, rounding up the people who did not come to the town square. They took what they wanted to eat and drink from the houses, and cuffed men, women, and children about with equal ferocity.

The contests and the killing continued. But somehow the people had grown numb, had shut away the specter of carnage from their minds. They could not look into the eyes of such horror, even as their brothers fell before them.

When the killing of the villagers did not accomplish his ends, El Muerte stopped the grisly affair and stood once again on the platform on which he had been seated.

"Is there no one to stand against me?"

The voice lifted above the crowd. But there was a stirring that ended almost as quickly as it had begun, and soon all eyes were turned toward El Muerte. Some of the soldiers backed away and avoided El Muerte's dreadful gaze. Others looked upon him in rapt fascination. El Muerte himself seemed to be searching for something as his gaze wandered over the top of the crowd that stood uneasily before him.

"Then bring the blind one," El Muerte said, not lifting his voice. The captain of the soldiers pushed three of his men roughly in the direction of El Muerte's camp, and when they had recovered their balance, they hurried to a small tent that was guarded heavily. When they returned, they pushed between them a small black man whose hands were bound behind him. Tarik looked and knew at once that it was Nongo.

Within the folds of his tunic, Tarik wiped his hands and placed his fingers around the handle of his sword. Before him the soldiers pushed Nongo forward and, at a gesture from El Muerte, placed him on the wagon.

"Whoever faces me and wins will get this black as his slave," El Muerte hissed between his teeth. His eyes were darkened slits that now lowered themselves onto the crowd.

Tarik bowed his head, as did the others in the crowd.

One of the soldiers unbound Nongo's hands and placed a wooden sword in it.

"Perhaps this will be your adversary!" the soldier called out. El Muerte did not look in the direction of Nongo, who let the sword drop by his side. He stood motionless and waited.

Tarik counted the soldiers who stood around El Muerte. There were twenty in all. If he eased his way toward the front of the crowd and drew close enough, he might yet rush El Muerte and plant his sword in his chest. If he was spotted, he would do well to save his own life, let alone that of Nongo, and he would have no chance to kill El Muerte.

Another of El Muerte's soldiers began to speak, calling the men of the village cowards and laughing at them. The men shifted uneasily. They had seen what happened to the man who had lifted his weapon against the soldiers.

Tarik glanced around and found himself looking into the eyes of Stria, who stood less than an arm's length from him. Her dark eyes smoldered as she stared at him. It was clear what she wanted to do. The tension in the crowd increased, and Tarik looked up to see El Muerte draw his sword. He put it along Nongo's neck. Every muscle in Tarik's body tensed as his mind raced wildly. He looked again at Stria, whose eyes had never left him.

"Look what rich blood he has." El Muerte's voice pulled Tarik's eyes back toward the wagon.

What he saw was El Muerte drawing his sword slowly across Nongo's shoulder. The cut was not deep enough to kill, but only to draw blood and to bring pain to the man. Blood now ran down the length of his arm.

Tarik could feel Stria's eyes on him. He looked at her again, this time against his will, and saw that she had unsheathed the dagger and had it gripped tightly in front of her, the knuckles of her hand white from the strength she put into the gripping of her instrument. Tarik looked around at the crowd; they had not noticed what the strange girl in their midst was doing. Instead they watched with fascination as El Muerte again drew his sword across Nongo's chest. The rage in Tarik welled in his throat, and he had withdrawn his own sword halfway from its sheath when he saw that Nongo, who had remained silent throughout his torture, now cupped his hand and caught his own blood. Then he poured the blood from one hand to the next and back again, letting no drops fall.

El Muerte saw this strange gesture and had the soldiers bind Nongo's hands. But Tarik had seen what Nongo had meant for him to see and remembered the lesson in the Gardens of Shange.

Tarik lowered his head and turned away. He felt tears stinging his eyes and falling down his cheeks. There was the sound of steel cutting through bone, a gasp and a few muffled cries from the crowd. Tarik, through his tears, looked once more into the dark eyes of Stria and turned away. The two fireballs had predicted two deaths, and now they had come to pass.

That night Capa gave Pen enough silver for another day's lodging and mentioned that they would not mind having a meal as delicious as the goat stew they had enjoyed the night before.

Pen took the silver and said he would see what he could do about a meal. Pen's wife, a thin woman who often mumbled to herself, took the silver from her husband and put it in her apron pocket.

"Come," Capa said to Tarik, "let us ride together and clear our heads as our friend prepares dinner for us."

But when they had left Pen's house, Capa quickly explained that he thought they should leave that very night.

"I do not trust him," Capa said. "He moves his eyes about too much. If we sleep another night in that place we might well dislike our awakening. What do you think?"

"I do not think," Tarik said. "My head is as empty as a drum. I saw Nongo die before my eyes and did not move from the spot."

"You could have done nothing more than you did, my friend," Capa said as he mounted his horse.

"What is right and what is wrong eludes me," Tarik said. "It slips between my fingers like handfuls of sand, falling even the more quickly as I grip what is left. I have forgotten why I set out upon this quest, or even why I stirred from my sleep this morning."

"You will remember," Capa answered. "You will remember. Now let us go."

"What about Stria? She did not return this evening."

"Do not worry about her," Capa said, spurring his horse on. "When we are long dead, those very eyes will still be disemboweling some man's dreams, believe me. I saw her leave, and she headed toward the road that leads from the village. Perhaps she will meet us along the way."

They did not see Stria along the road but found her near the cypress stand beyond the gate. Stria stepped from the shadows and frightened Capa nearly out of his mind. The round man pulled clumsily at his sword and shouted into the wind until he saw that it was the girl.

"My precious Lord!" Capa put his hand to his chest as if to prevent his pounding heart from bursting through it.

Stria ignored him and stood in front of Tarik, blocking his path to Zinzinbadio.

Her eyes, even in the brilliant moonlight, seemed deeper than ever. She did not wear the shawl around her now, but stood instead, bare-legged in the short leather tunic that Tarik had first seen in the Gardens of Shange. Her hair, which she had worn long, was tied back, revealing the firmness of her jaw and the long arc of her neck.

"You asked me to wait while you struck the first blow," she said, "and you did not even lift your hand."

"The blow will be struck soon," Tarik said. "And if you follow my footsteps you will see it struck."

"So be it," Stria said, "but ask nothing of me, for I have nothing more to grant you."

161

They rode all night along the road leading southward from Olcades and then westward until they reached a small village near the town in Oretani called Libis. It had been a long journey for Tarik, and by the time they could see the morning breaking across the sky, he felt as if he had been traveling all his life. Capa rode ahead of him, his head hunched into his shoulders, and behind him were the accusing eyes of Stria. Tarik knew that she had grown weary of the waiting even as Tarik had grown weary of the killing. Now, even with the pain he felt at the loss of Docao and Nongo, he could not bring himself to lust for the death of El Muerte. But it was a thing that must be done, he knew, if it was to be put forever behind him. He had no wife to go home to, as Capa did, nor did he share the single madness of Stria's unfulfilled vision that would make the completion of his task a thing of joy.

Many had died at his hand, and still there was one more to whom he must bring death. Perhaps, he thought, he must die himself. But where could he hide from the nightmare visions of his father's thin black arm held high to ward off the terrible blow that ended his life? What ocean could roar loudly enough to close from his ears the sound of his brother's last desperate cry? Tarik hung his head, and for all the greatness of the horse between his thighs, the sword that hung from his side, and the Crystal in the pouch around his neck, he longed only for the forgetfulness of sleep.

SIXTEEN

WHEN THEY REACHED LIBIS, THEY DISCOVERED IT TO be a small village of craftsmen who often traveled to nearby towns to sell their wares. After their horses had been watered and were resting, a plan came to Tarik and he spoke of it to Capa.

"No," Capa said. "I don't like this plan. It has too many things that can go wrong. It is too dangerous. Have I told you that I am a coward?"

"Yes," Tarik answered, "but you are still with me, my friend."

Tarik knew that his plan was not without faults, but he also knew he must act at once or grow too weary of soul to act at all. He spoke to Stria, telling her of the plan, as he had told Capa. Again he asked her to wait until he was ready to strike and took her silence for a guarded assent.

They found lodging in the back of a potter's shop, and Tarik had Capa make a big show of being very busy. This Capa did, walking about the small village at a quick pace, pretending to examine this thing and the next, and then scurrying back to where Tarik spent his hours thinking of what he must do and where Stria sharpened her weapons.

Next Capa and Tarik went to a fine carpenter and asked him to fashion a box in which to bury a large person.

"It must be at least four and a half cubits long and two cubits wide," Capa said, "and nicely carved with the figure of a flying bird."

"Poof!" The carpenter twisted his face in disapproval. "I don't do my work to have it buried in the ground!"

"You will do as you are told," Tarik said, drawing his sword, "or this town will have need for someone else to work its wood."

"And one end must be tapered, as is the style," Capa continued. "And the joints must fit nicely without filling them with clay. I will look for this, so be careful. And the bottom must have a piece of cedar, so that it smells nice."

"Who is this huge god you bury?" the craftsmen asked.

"It is not a god," Tarik answered gruffly. "Just do as you are told, or it is you who will fill the box."

There were two silver workers in the town, and to one of them Capa gave the task of fashioning a shrouded hawk, and to the other he gave the task of fashioning the letters to spell out "El Muerte."

"So that they join on the bottom," Capa said. "But you must not talk about what you are doing to anyone, upon penalty of death. Do you understand that?"

The silversmith said that he did and set about his task.

Then Capa went to a priest and asked if he could say a few prayers over a very important person on the night of the full moon. The priest, a holy and pious man, said that he would.

The last thing Capa did was buy a goat. When the carpenter had finished the box, Capa had him cover it with a great deal of heavy linen and bring it to a field. Then he spent all of a morning measuring off a distance. The people of Libis watched him with amusement, and some, who had seen him speak to the carpenter, asked what was under the linen.

"I am bound not to speak of it," the carpenter answered them.

When Capa had finished marking off the distance that he wanted, he asked if anyone came to the field at night and was told no. Then he asked the man from whom he had bought the goat to bring the goat to the field that night.

When the sun had set, Capa tied the goat near the burying box. Then he paced off the same distance that he had that morning and marked the place with his cap, pretending not to see the many eyes that watched from the trees. Then he looked around and gave a signal. When the townspeople turned, they saw Tarik astride Zinzinbadio. Tarik clucked his tongue in the horse's ear, and the horse sped across the field, moving faster than anything that the startled townspeople had ever seen. With a single movement Tarik leaned from the saddle and cut the goat in two and was off into the gathering darkness.

Capa took the goat and drained its blood into the burying box, making a great show of checking all the corners to see that they did not leak. This done, he covered the box again and had the carpenter take it back and conceal it in his shop.

"On the day of the first full moon, I will have need for it," Capa said. "Until then you must not speak a word."

Tongues clacked noisily the next morning in the small market. There were many strange things going on in the town. From somewhere a stranger had come and had a huge burying box built and had had the name of El Muerte fashioned in silver. And there was, too, a strange knight who rode like a fleeting shadow across the field and killed with uncommon skill.

The story was told and told again and went from field to field and from house to house. Someone would be buried on the night of the full moon. And the name that fell haltingly from the lips was that of El Muerte.

When the story had traveled throughout the town, it went on eager lips in all directions, and even to Olcades.

When the rumor reached Olcades, it did so by way of a merchant, an otherwise wise man who dealt in many types of goods, who was brought before the captain of the guard. When he had told his story, he was then brought before El Muerte himself.

The captain of the guard explained to El Muerte that he had seen many people leaving Olcades and had questioned them, and what story they had related.

"They say," the captain said, "that there will be a great funeral in Libis on the first day of the full moon. This dog has sold the linen to wrap the body. Already a box has been prepared to bury the body and the name affixed to it in fine silver. The box is lined with cedar and has been tested with goat's blood so that it does not spill the vitals of the one who has died."

"And what great person lives among these pigs to have his name in silver?" El Muerte asked, his eyes closed as Jad and another slave combed and oiled his hair.

The captain looked at the merchant uneasily, not wishing to repeat the name that he had heard from the man. But he also knew that he must give El Muerte an answer.

"He will not say the name, sire," the captain said.

"Then kill him," El Muerte said quietly.

"Sire, have mercy!" The merchant fell to his knees. "I have a wife and four sons who have loved you all their lives, even as I have loved you from the first time that I heard the sound of your name. I say again what I have heard—that it is El Muerte they bury, and that it is the black one who has killed him. May the gods strike me dead and curse the birthright of my sons if this is not true, sire."

"There was another who allowed this same gibberish to fall from his lips, sire," the captain of the guard said. "We beat him until he did not remember the name his mother cursed him with, and he speaks no more of such evil."

"What does this other man do?" El Muerte asked, pushing away the slave who braided his hair.

"Nothing of note, sire," the captain of the guard replied. "He, like this man, is a stupid seller of goods."

"What goods does he sell?"

"Candles, sire," was the reply.

When El Muerte had heard this, he told the captain of the guard to have the merchant beaten to see if he changed his story, or until death came to him. Then he bade Jad the Unclean come to him and read his fortune.

Jad the Unclean had also heard the story of the funeral in Libis. It had been spread throughout the village of Olcades, and many had come to look to see if it was true that El Muerte was really dead.

When El Muerte bade him read his fortune, he brought his bones and cast them three times, each time shaking his head and grunting, as was his habit when doing such things.

"What do the bones say?" El Muerte asked.

"They do not speak, for there is no truth in that which is being passed from ear to ear," Jad said. "It is the talk of foolish people. El Muerte lives and will live forever!"

"Then why do they say that I have been killed by the black one?" El Muerte asked. "This thing must have a meaning put to it."

Jad the Unclean cast the bones again. This time he cast them five times, each time faster than the time before, snatching them up from the dusty floor, rubbing them in the spittle he placed in the palm of his hand, and casting them in great concern again.

Then he drew a circle in the dirt. He placed one hand in the circle, cast the bones within the same arc, and spun himself around them until he reached the place from where he had begun his stunted dance.

"It is a joke of the gods," Jad said, recovering. "Look, El Muerte is so great that the gods smile on him and pull his beard. It shows the greatness of El Muerte."

Then Jad the Unclean fell on his knees before El Muerte

and kissed his feet. El Muerte looked down at him and laughed; then he kicked Jad away from him and sat silently, staring at the bones that lay in the circle. Two of them had threes up, he noticed, and this was not a good thing.

"Could this black one be the spirit of the blacks I have killed?" El Muerte asked Jad.

"Then it is he who is to be buried," said Jad.

"The black one?"

"None other," Jad answered. "It is he who is dead and El Muerte who lives."

"Then it is not a joke of the gods?"

"It is a joke that the gods play on El Muerte, for he is as great as they."

"I think I will have you killed soon," El Muerte said. "You are too ugly to live. Perhaps later I will have you split open like the pig you are and eat you."

Jad whimpered like a dog and rolled along the floor before El Muerte, licking his shoes and kissing his heels. El Muerte looked at this for a while and then again kicked him away.

That night he had his best horseman ride with two fine animals to Libis to see if they still made preparations for his funeral. The rider rode all night and arrived in Libis that next morning before the sun rose. He awakened some goat herders who kept flocks near the edge of the village and asked them about the funeral. They told him that a great number of people had been promised a piece of silver each to mourn for the dead man. When the rider asked whose body was to be buried, the goat herder said that they were not told, but that there would be great rejoicing if the name the wind carried was correct.

"Has any man seen the body?" the rider asked, as he had been instructed to.

"No one has seen the body, for it is a great secret," the goat herder declared. "The Prince does not want the people to know the truth. But the silver that is offered the mourners is more truth than the eye carries."

Armed with this knowledge, the rider leaped on the back of the second horse and rode back to Olcades, stopping neither to eat nor drink until he had gained the presence of El Muerte himself.

He related what the goat herder had told him, and the news brought a rage to El Muerte that made those around him tremble.

"What stupidity!" He screamed the words at the rider and struck that unfortunate across the face with his whip. "Do you think I am dead?"

"No, sire." The rider's lips trembled as he spoke, for he knew each breath might be his very last.

"Then why do they do these things?"

"They are fools," the rider said, his eyes downcast.

"And did you tell them that I live?"

"The very words," the rider replied, "but the silver they have been promised speaks to their stupid hearts, while my words . . ."

El Muerte did not wait to hear the rest of what the rider said. He turned away sharply and sat next to the fire that had been built. The captain of the guard began to flog the rider, and did so until they had moved out of sight of El Muerte.

"Get me a fool!" El Muerte demanded.

Several soldiers quickly took this demand to the captain of the guard who, in turn, sent for the old man who cleaned the stables. When he had been brought to the captain, he was carefully examined and told what to say.

"If he asks if you are a fool, say that indeed you are!" the captain said. "If you do not say that you are a fool, I will have your entrails cut out and fed to the crows. Do you understand me?"

"I do that," the stable cleaner said, cowering under the captain's glance.

"If you do, after all, have another half of a wit, you will be very wise not to discover it any time soon. Now, come along with you."

The captain grabbed the man by the collar and dragged him to where El Muerte waited, reporting that the man was the fool requested.

"Fool"—El Muerte closed one eye, lifted his head, and looked down at the man with the other slitted eye—"what would you do if you heard suddenly that you were being buried in another town?"

"I would go to see it, sire," the man said, bowing slightly as he did so.

"And why would you do that?"

"Because it would be the wise thing to do, sire," was the quick response. A sharp pain clutched at the man's stomach as the words came out. He shot a glance over to where the captain stood grinding his teeth.

"Well said." El Muerte waved the man away. "He is indeed a fool. See that he is taken care of so that I may use him again when I have need of a fool."

The captain of the guard motioned the man away and approached El Muerte.

"I thought he was a good fool, sire. I have never known him to say anything that was not the utterance of a fool."

"Am I a fool?"

"No, sire."

"A fool would go to Libis to look at the funeral. Curiosity compels the fool, sucks at his marrow, draws him along like a monkey on a cord."

"Yes, sire."

"Why is it that we know so much about this funeral? It is a big secret, they say, and yet every dog that has a tail is wagging it. Let us make them think that El Muerte is a fool. We will go into their trap with our eyes wide and our hands shaking. We will go into their trap, and then, when we are discovered and the trap is sprung about us, we will spring ours about them.

"They plan to have the funeral in an open field—that's where they would meet us. But it must be that the black one has found an army among the men of Libis. I will go to the field with a small escort. But just before I arrive at the field, you will have your soldiers attack their village. When they hear the screams of their wives and babes, they will soon desert the black one. Then we will have him."

"It's a good plan, sire." The captain of the guard nodded. "Very good."

The captain of the guard and his sergeant rode abreast slowly as they passed the sparse grove of lemon trees that marked the boundaries of Libis; behind them rode El Muerte. All wore capes to conceal their battle garb. The cloud-streaked moon played shadows across El Muerte's grimly waxen face, making him appear to be more thing than man. Behind El Muerte rode Jad the Unclean, bareback on a high-spirited gray gelding. They had ridden the better part of the previous night and the morning that followed and had then rested until the sun had set in the evening. Then they had mounted their steeds for the last part of their journey.

It had been planned that, once they reached the village, the captain of the guard would sound a horn, signaling an attack on the village. When the men of the village went to defend their homes, El Muerte would then enter the field where the funeral was scheduled to take place.

"Suppose the black one doesn't remain in the field?" the sergeant asked out of earshot of El Muerte. "Suppose he goes and helps to defend the village?"

"It makes little difference," the captain said. "If he fights in the village, our men have been instructed to turn their attention solely to killing him. Even if he stands alone in the field, then El Muerte himself will take the honor."

"I hope it goes as planned," the sergeant said. "I don't want to have to face this black knight if he's half as terrible as what's being whispered."

"Can you imagine him a greater or more powerful fighter than El Muerte?"

"That's true, my friend, but it is not El Muerte's hide I worry about. El Muerte sends his entire army to ferret out this knight while the two of us ride lonely escort to him and that white monkey of his. It's my own hide I worry about."

"Better not worry too loudly, my friend," the captain replied. "Look, there is the field, and I see people gathered there in the corner."

"Hardly an army."

"No, but still we'll put the plan into effect."

SEVENTEEN

TARIK HAD NOT RESTED WELL THAT DAY. AGAIN AND again he had played out the scene in his mind. He would stand face to face with El Muerte, and they would settle with their swords the debt that lay between them. Tarik had often thought of this moment and had wondered if he would have the courage to stand against the man who had once crushed his spirit with terror. But now he felt no terror; no fear rumbled about his bowels. He felt, if anything, a calmness, almost a sadness. As Capa busied himself making the final arrangements for the mock funeral, Tarik rested against the gnarled trunk of an old oak tree. Zinzinbadio nuzzled at his shoulder. Even the horse seemed more tense than usual, and Tarik, from time to time, whispered soothingly in the beast's ear.

Tarik knew that El Muerte was a great fighter, and he had been warned by Nongo of the strength of the evil possessed by the man. Tarik closed his eyes and tried to shut out the thought that lay on his mind like early morning dew: his hope that El Muerte would not come. But he knew in his heart that El Muerte would come, bringing with him the moment when Tarik's spirit would either flame into nothingness across the vast night sky, as had the spirits of Nongo and Docao, or would brighten the sky and live with the glory of a new day. And to this grand moment Tarik could bring only the death that Serq would wield, and a fading echo of a distant righteousness.

"What is your choice, black friend?" Stria had asked him.

Tarik lifted himself from his brooding and went over to where Capa stood wringing his hands. Capa the baker was a man whose very fear enhanced his bravery, Tarik thought.

Across the road Stria sat cross-legged like a street beggar in the darkness. Earlier, when he had spoken to her of his plans, she had simply turned away. It was enough for her to know that El Muerte might come. Beyond that there was no reason that would touch her.

"There, that's the funeral!" The sergeant spoke softly. "Look at them. What devil's child do they bury in the middle of the night? I don't like it—they could be witches. I'm glad I'm wearing a garlic clove around my neck. Are you wearing one?"

"I don't believe in such nonsense," the captain retorted. "Garlic is good for the flux and little else. I gave silver to a dealer in spells. I am well protected."

"Sound the alarm before they see us."

The captain raised the horn to his lips and sounded three long notes, two high and one much lower. Immediately there was the sound of shouting from the village and the sounding of more horns.

"The village is being attacked!" The cry went up and was repeated. The people Capa had hired for the funeral, one moment gravely solemn and the next in panic, began to flee across the field toward the sounds of battle. A fat man, his long mourning robes flapping furiously, fell over Stria in the darkness. He got up, cursing and clawing his way through the bushes, and followed the others.

Capa had fallen, too, and Tarik pulled him quickly to his feet. No sooner had he done so than the sound of hoofbeats were upon them. Tarik drew Serq and turned to see riders dismounting. They were soldiers. They drew their swords, turning them toward Capa, who stumbled to where he had rested his own weapon. Tarik started to move to help Capa, but was fixed to the spot as his eyes met those of a huge figure on a white horse. El Muerte.

He thought for the space of a wink of mounting Zinzinbadio so that he might be of equal height with El Muerte, but then thought better of it. He came quickly from the shadows toward El Muerte's side. Something came at him, something white and small. There was a flash, and Tarik brought his sword in front of himself just in time to hear the clashing of steel against steel. He crashed headlong over the white thing that had attacked him, landing heavily on his chest, and rolled over onto his back. Above him El Muerte's horse reared high into the night air before him, and the two soldiers who had accosted Capa now closed in behind him.

Tarik's sword was still at hand but beneath his body. As the sergeant lifted his sword, there was a great scream that did not sound human. But the bare-legged figure that came from the shadows, plunging her dagger deep into the heart of the sergeant, was very human. It was Stria.

Stria pulled her blade from the chest of the mortally wounded soldier as he fell. She whirled just quickly enough to divert the arc of the captain's sword from its deadly path toward her own bosom. As Tarik struggled to his feet, he saw that Capa had joined the fray, attacking with a vengeance the little man who had set upon Tarik at the outset of the fight. Tarik looked up and saw El Muerte sitting calmly on his horse. The muscles in the huge man's face moved, and his face fell into a smile as he saw Tarik standing before him on the ground.

As the sounds of the battles between Stria and the captain and Capa and Jad the Unclean raged around them, El Muerte and Tarik were frozen in the moon's silver light.

El Muerte swung slowly from his horse, hanging interminably in the stirrup before slapping the horse with the broadside of his sword and driving it into Tarik. Tarik sprang to one side quickly, and brought his sword hard against the thrust of El Muerte. For a moment they stood together, matching strength against strength, until El Muerte began to prevail and Tarik backed away.

Tarik had faced no one with the strength or skill of El Muerte. The blows from the great sword El Muerte carried came faster and faster, each one making Tarik's arm tremble with its force. El Muerte rained the blows down on Tarik, forcing him backward and then to one knee, but still no blow went through Tarik's defenses. But Tarik knew that it would be only a matter of time unless he did something quickly. He began to parry El Muerte's blows with greater and greater force, hoping for some relenting of his grinning foe, or at least some mistake in his attack. But there was none. Tarik realized that El Muerte knew that he could not break Tarik's guard with speed, for there was no place he twisted the sword that it was not watched, but his great strength was a different matter. And if either Capa or Stria was defeated, all would be lost.

Tarik allowed El Muerte's blows to come closer to his body until he could hear their singing in his ears. If he had held a weapon other than the marvelous Serq, he would have already been dead.

El Muerte, seeing that his sword was nearing the mark and sensing that the end was near, shifted his feet so that he could strike his blows with even greater strength. But in the moment between the movement of the foot and the lifting of the sword, Tarik managed to step backward and regain his own solid footing, and the two stood facing each other, their breaths coming in great heaves.

"Your death will bring much honor to me, fool!" El Muerte twisted in rage as he spoke.

"Words fall away on the wind," Tarik replied. "And they are the only wounds you have dealt me thus far."

El Muerte swung his sword with a great vengeance, and Tarik caught its full strength on his own and staggered back, his ears ringing from the deadly clash. The next blow was as strong, and the image that Tarik had seen in the Crystal came to mind. Tarik knew what he must do.

As the next blow was delivered, he caught it as close to his body as he could, allowing El Muerte to expend more of his energy without exchanging his life in the bargain. But the moment the force had been expended, Tarik made a thrust of his own and stepped backward. The point of Serq had caught El Muerte's side, and the huge man brought his elbow to the offended spot.

El Muerte continued the attack, but for every blow he struck, Tarik managed to thrust at him and find some small opening. Then, suddenly, the expression in El Muerte's eyes changed from anger to delight. His eyes flickered to a spot behind Tarik. The thought occurred to Tarik that it was either the captain that Stria had fought or the white thing—Jad—that Capa had engaged. El Muerte came now with a fury, screaming as he did so.

"Get him! Get him!"

But Tarik had already reached beyond himself and had felt nothing close enough to strike a blow. Instead of turning, he watched El Muerte's sword, saw him change his grip on the handle. This time he stepped forward, catching the weapon on his own before it had gained full force. He slid his own weapon along that of his enemy and thrust his sword with all his strength into the exposed neck before him.

El Muerte staggered backward, a look of utter surprise on his face. He reached for his neck and withdrew a bloody hand. Now, a man possessed, he once again attacked Tarik. Never before had the blows been more vicious. Each one made Tarik's body tremble with their force. There was no time to recover to attack El Muerte again. Tarik went backward from the blows and then down to the ground. El Muerte, the blood pouring from his neck and running down the front of his tunic, stood over him, beating down on him with his sword as if he were a woodsman felling an oak. But soon the blows came more slowly, and it was with less force that they landed upon Serq. Tarik's arms had scarcely the strength left to ward off even these weak blows. Then El Muerte lifted his sword for one final effort. He held it high above his head, lifted his head to the heavens, and fell backward, dead.

"At last it is finished," Tarik said to the darkness around him. Images of his father and his mother and of his brothers ran through his mind. Images, too, of Docao and of Nongo. There was a clap of thunder, and it began to rain lightly. Tarik looked over to where El Muerte's body lay, and saw the rain already cleansing the dark stains from the earth.

Tarik looked around him and saw that Capa and Jad the Unclean were still dueling, but more with words than with actions as they cautiously circled each other and made timid thrusts. He looked once again and finally saw Stria astride the captain, striking at him with her dagger. Tarik pushed himself up to go to her assistance, his legs still trembling from his mighty efforts against El Muerte. But as he approached her, he saw that she needed no help. The captain of the guard was quite dead, and her fury was spent in vain as she plunged her dagger into him again and again.

"Stria." He called her name softly. "Stria, it is over. El Muerte is dead."

She came back to him as if awaking from a dream. The knife that had made its deadly arc in the dimming moonlight slowed, and she turned to him. There was blood on her face, and her dark eyes seemed sightless. She looked again at the soldier, spat upon his carcass, and lifted herself away from him.

"Stria, are you all right?" Tarik asked.

"Have you killed him?" she asked, ignoring the question, as was her custom.

"I have."

When they turned their attention to Capa, he had ended his fight with Jad. The little man had given up and now lay quivering at Capa's feet.

"What shall we do with this one?" Capa asked, his foot on Jad's neck.

"Kill him!" Stria said.

"There's no need for more killing," Tarik said. "It sickens me to see what has happened to us."

"Kill him," Stria said again, her voice more of a growl this time.

"I will not allow it," Tarik said. "Tie him up."

Tarik and Stria lay on the cool earth beneath the branches of a tree as Capa tied Jad to its trunk upside down. They rested from their efforts as best they could in the coolness of the evening, minding neither the gentle rain nor their own weariness.

No thought came to Tarik. There was no sweetness in his victory over El Muerte, no satisfaction in the vengeance gained. In the field before him small birds flittered about the bodies of the dead. Tarik looked at the large carcass of

El Muerte and wondered if there existed elsewhere in the world a beast so evil.

It was Capa who slept first. Tarik watched as his friend breathed heavily in his rest.

"Stria," he said, turning to the girl, "I owe you more than I can say. For now that this is done with, perhaps I will be able to live again among people.

"I am Tarik," he said, taking the amulet his father had given him from around his neck. He held it in his hand, kissed it, and then put it around Stria's neck. "As long as my name lives among my people, it will be a name that is a friend to those who bear yours."

For a long time the girl did not speak, or acknowledge Tarik's hand upon hers. Then, after he had taken his hand away, she spoke.

"I am Stria," she said. "If I had a kind word in my mouth, I would give it to you. But they have been taken from me."

"We cannot go on holding bitterness in our hearts, Stria," Tarik said. "What is done is done."

But the girl had already turned away.

Tarik did not remember when he fell asleep; he knew only that the sun was high when he awoke. There was a buzzing nearby, and he saw a ring of townspeople standing at the edge of the field. For some reason he looked over to where El Muerte lay, to see if he was still dead or if the killing itself had been a dream. But the evil one still lay there, as ugly in death as he had been in life.

"Hello!" Capa spoke. "I have fed the horses with gifts from the townspeople. They say the news of your having killed El Muerte already travels, and that people will bring you more gifts."

"I have the gift of whatever days I have left on the earth," Tarik said. "It is enough. It is time that I sought my people and my home. My river sends its sweet smell across the earth, and the sound of distant drums calls for me."

"Aye," Capa said, "and I must find my fat wife before the weather cools."

"And Stria?" Tarik asked. "Where is she?"

"Stand and you will see her," Capa said, pointing to the east. "I think she waits for you to rise."

Tarik stood and saw silhouetted against the sky a figure on horseback in the distance. When he stood, the figure waved, turned the horse, and went off over the mountain.

"Let us go, too," Capa said. "I don't trust gifts."

"Have we decided what to do with the little one?" Tarik asked.

"The girl decided in the night, my friend," Capa said.

Tarik looked to where they had tied Jad the Unclean, and saw that he would speak no more or do more evil.

Zinzinbadio's back felt good, even to Tarik's aching body. He turned the great horse to where he thought Al-kebu-lan might lie and urged him forward.

He had come to this strange land a frightened boy, full of the dreams of the new day that lit every young life, and now he left it with much weight on his shoulders and much in his heart. The people of the town cheered him as he left and some brought gifts for him to take along on his journey. He looked once more at Capa, his brave and true friend, and in the direction that the strange Stria had ridden, and then freed his mind from all thoughts.

It was said that three times they tried to bury El Muerte, and three times the earth cast his body up. For years it was whispered that his spirit still roamed the field on which he died.

But it was said, too, that there was a great knight who had come from somewhere to the south, and that the knight was tall and as black as ebony. And that wherever the spirit of El Muerte went, the knight would find and destroy it, and as long as that was so, Evil would not conquer Good. For many years thereafter the people of Libis called the first day of spring The Day of the Black Knight. They would celebrate the day with great and sumptuous feasts and the telling of all the marvelous deeds that Tarik had done.

About the Author

Walter Dean Myers is the author of many magazine arti-
cles and works of short fiction. He has also written many
novels for young adults, among them three ALA Notable
Books: *Fast Sam, Cool Clyde, and Stuff, It Ain't All for
Nothin'*, and *The Young Landlords*. His most recent book for
Viking is *The Golden Serpent*, illustrated by Alice and Mar-
tin Provensen. Mr. Myers lives in New Jersey.